The Stolen Mask; or, The Mysterious Cash-Box

Wilkie Collins

THE STOLEN MASK;
OR THE
MYSTERIOUS CASH-BOX.

A STORY FOR A CHRISTMAS FIRESIDE.

BY

WILKIE COLLINS

1864.

INTRODUCTION.

It may possibly happen that some of the readers of this story have in their possession a plaster "mask"—or, face and forehead—of Shakspeare, which is a cast from the celebrated Stratford bust. These casts were first offered for sale some time since. The circumstances under which the original mould was taken, I heard thus related by a friend, (now no more,) to whose affectionate remembrance of me I am indebted for the specimen of the mask which I now possess:

A stone-mason at Stratford-upon-Avon was employed, a few years ago, to make repairs in the church. While thus engaged, he managed—as he thought, unsuspected—to make a mould from the Shakspeare bust. What he had done was found out, however; and he was forthwith threatened, by the authorities having care of the bust, with the severest pains and penalties of the law—though for what especial offence was not specified. The poor man was so frightened at these menaces, that he packed up his tools at once, and, taking the mould with him, left Stratford. Having afterwards stated his case to persons competent to advise him, he was told that he need fear no penalty whatever, and that if he thought he could dispose of them, he might make as many casts as he pleased, and offer them for sale anywhere. He took the advice, placed his masks neatly on slabs of black marble, and sold great numbers of them, not only in England, but in America also. It should be added, that this stonemason had been always remarkable for his extraordinary reverence of Shakspeare, which he carried to such an extent as to assure the friend from whom I derived the information here given, that if (as a widower) he ever married again, it should be only when he could meet with a woman who was a lineal descendant of William Shakspeare!

From the anecdote I have related, the first idea of the following pages was derived. I now offer my little book to the public, in writing which I have endeavored to tell a simple story, simply and familiarly; or, in other words, as if I were only telling it to an audience of friends at my own fireside.

WILKIE COLLINS.

HANOVER TERRACE, REGENT'S PARK.

CHAPTER I.

ELOCUTION FOR THE MILLION.

I should be insulting the intelligence of readers generally, if I thought it at all necessary to describe to them that widely-celebrated town, Tidbury-on-the-Marsh. As a genteel provincial residence, who is unacquainted with it? The magnificent new hotel that has grown on to the side of the old inn; the extensive library, to which, not satisfied with only adding new books, they are now adding a new entrance as well; the projected crescent of palatial abodes in the Grecian style, on the top of the hill, to rival the completed erescent of castellated abodes, in the Gothic style, at the bottom of the hill—are not such local objects as these perfectly well known to any intelligent Englishman? Of course they are! The question is superfluous. Let us get on at once, without wasting more time, from Tidbury in general to the High Street in particular, and to our present destination there—the commercial establishment of Messrs. Dunball and Dark.

Looking merely at the colored liquids, the miniature statue of a horse, the corn-plasters, the oil-skin bags, the pots of cosmetics, and the cut-glass saucers full of lozenges in the shop-window, you might at first imagine that Dunball and Dark were only chemists. Looking carefully through the entrance, towards an inner apartment, an inscription; a large, upright mahogany receptacle, or box, with a hole in it; brass rails protecting the hole; a green curtain ready to draw over the hole; and a man with a copper money-shovel in his hand, partially visible behind the hole—would be sufficient to inform you that Dunball and Dark were not chemists only, but "Branch Bankers" as well.

It is a rough, squally morning at the end of November. Mr. Dunball (in the absence of Mr. Dark, who has gone to make a speech at the Vestry Meeting,) has got into the mahogany box, and has assumed the whole business and direction of the Branch Bank. He is a very fat man, and looks absurdly over large for his sphere of action. Not a single customer has, as yet, applied for money—nobody has come even to gossip with the Branch Banker through the brass rails of his commercial prison-house. There he sits, staring calmly through the chemical part of the shop into the street—his gold in one drawer, his notes in another, his elbows on his ledgers, his copper shovel under his thumb; the picture of monied loneliness; the hermit of British finance.

In the outer shop is the young assistant, ready to drug the public at a moment's notice. But Tidbury-on-the-Marsh is an unprofitably healthy place, and no public appears. By the time the young assistant has ascertained from the shop clock that it is a quarter past 10, and from the weather-cock opposite that the wind is "Sou'-sou'-west," he has exhausted all external sources of amusement, and is reduced to occupying himself by first sharpening his pen-knife, and then cutting his nails. He has completed his left hand, and has just begun on the right hand thumb, when a customer actually darkens the shop-door at Iast!

Mr. Dunball starts, and grasps the copper shovel; the young assistant shuts up his pen-knife in a hurry, and makes a bow. The customer is a young girl, and she has come for a pot of lip-salve.

She is very neatly and quietly dressed; looks about eighteen or nineteen years of age; and has something in her face which I can only characterize by the epithet—lovable. There is a beauty of innocence and purity about her forehead, brow and eyes—a calm, kind, happy expression as she looks at you—and a curious, home-sonnd in her clear utterance when she speaks, which, altogether, make you fancy, stranger as you are, that you must have known her and loved her long ago, and somehow or other ungratefully forgotten her in the lapse of time. Mlixed up, however, with the girlish gentleness and innocence which form her more proininent charm, there is a look of firmness—especially noticeable about the expression of her lips— that gives a certain charaeter and originality to her face. Her figure—

I stop at her figure. Not by any means for want of phrases to describe it; but from a disheartening conviction of the powerlessness of any description of her at all to produce the right effect on the minds of others. If I were asked in what particular efforts of literature the poverty of literary material most remarkably appears, I should answer, in personal descriptions of heroines. We have all read these by the hundred—some of them so carefully and finely finished, that we are not only informed about the lady's eyes, eye-brows, nose, cheeks, complexion, mouth, teeth, neck, ears, head, hair and the way it was dressed; but are also made acquainted with the particular manner in which the sentiments below made the bosom above heave or swell; besides the exact position of head in which her eye-lashes were just long enough to cast a shadow on her cheeks. We have read all this attentively and admiringly, as it deserves; and have yet risen from the reading, without the remotest approach to a realization in our own minds of what sort of a woman the heroine really was. We vaguely knew she was beautiful, at the beginning of the description; and we know just as much—just as vaguely—at the end.

Penetrated with the conviction above mentioned, I prefer leaving the reader (assisted by a striking likeness in the frontispiece) to form his own realization of the personal appelrance of the customer at Messers. Dunball and Dark's. Eschewing the magnificent beauties of his acquaintance, let him imagine her to be like any pretty, intelligent girl whom he knows—any of those pleasant little fire-side angels, who can charm us even in a merino morning gown, darning an old pair of socks. Let this be the sort of female reality in the reader's mind; and neither author nor heroine need have any reason to complain.

Well; our young lady came to the counter, and asked for lip-salve. The assistant, vanquished at once by the potent charm of her presence, paid her the first little tribute of politeness in his power, by asking permission to send the gallipot home for her.

"I beg your pardon, miss," said he; "but I think you live lower down, at No. 12. I was passing, and I think I saw you going in there, yesterday, with an old gentleman and another gentleman. I think I did, miss?"

"Yes; we lodge at No. 12," said the young girl; "but I will take the lip-salve home with me, if you please. I have a favor, however, to ask of you before I go," she continued, very modestly, but without the slightest appearance of embarrassment; "if you have room to hang this up in your window, my grand-father, Mr. Wray, would feel much obliged by your kindness."

And here, to the utter astonishment of the young assistant, she handed him a piece of card-board, with a string to hang it up by, on which appeared the following inscription, neatly written:

"Mr. Reuben Wray, pupil of the late celebrated John Kemble, Esquire, begs respectfully to inform his friends and the public that he gives Iessons in elocution, delivery and reading aloud, price two-and-sixpenee the lesson of an hour. Pupils prepared for the stage, or private theatricals, on a principle combining intelligent interpretation of the text, with the action of the arms and legs adopted by the late illustrious Roscius of the English stage, J. Kemble, Esquire; and attentively studied from cIose observation of Mr. J. K. by Mr. R. W. Orators and clergymen improved, (with the strictest secresy,) at three-and-sixpence the lesson of an hour. Impediments and hesitation of utterance combated and removed. Young ladies taught the graces of delivery, and young gentlemen the proprieties of diction. A discount allowed to schools and large classes. Please to address Mr. Reuben Wray (late of the Theatre Royal, Drury Laue,) 12 High street, Tidbury-on-the-Marsh."

No Babylonian inscription that ever was cut, no manuscript on papyrus that ever was penned, could possibly have puzzled the young assistant more than this remarkable advertisement. He read it all through in a state of stupefaction; and then observed, with a bewildered look at the young girl on the other side of the counter:

"Very nicely written, miss; and very nicely composed indeed! I suppose—in fact, I'm sure Mr. Dunball"—Here a creaking was heard, as of some strong wooden construction being gradually rent asunder. It was Mr. Dunball himself, squeezing his way out of the Branch Bank box, and coming to examine the advertisement.

He read it all through very attentively, following each line with his forefinger; and then cautiously and gently laid the card-board down on the counter. When I state that neither Mr. Dunball nor his assistant were quite certain what a "Roscius of the the English stage" meant, or what precise branch of human attainment Mr. Wray designed to teach in teaching "elocution," I do no injustice either to master or man.

"So you want this. bung up in the window, my—in the window, miss?" asked Mr. Dunball. He was about to say, "my dear;" but something in the girl's look and manner stopped him.

"If you could hang it without inconvenience, sir."

"May I ask what's your name? and where you come from?"

"My name is Annie Wray; and the last place we came from was Stratford-upon-Avon."

"Ah! indeed—and Mr. Wray teaches, does he?—elocution for half a crown—eh?"

"My grand-father only desires to let the inhabitants of this place know that he can teach those who wish it, to speak or read with a good delivery and a proper pronunciation."

Mr. Dauball feh rather puzzled by the straight-forward, self-possessed manner in which he—a branch banker, chemist, and a municipal authority—was answered by little Annie Wray. He took up the advertisement again; and walked away to read it a second time in the solemn monetary seclusion of the back shop.

The young assistant followed. "I think they're respectable people, sir," said he, in a whisper; "I was passing when the old gentlermin went into No. 12, yesterday. The wind blew his cloak on one side, and I saw him carrying a large cash-box under it—I did indeed, sir; and it seemed a heavy one."

"Cash-box!" cried Mr. Dunball. "What does a man with a cash box want with elocution, and two-and-sixpence an hour? Suppose he should be a swindler!"

"He can't be, sir; look at the young lady! Besides, the people at No. 12 told me he gave a reference, and paid a week's rent in advance."

"He did—did he? I say, are you sure it was a cash-box?"

"Certain, sir. I suppose it had money in it, of course?"

"What's the use of a cash-box, without cash?" said the Branch Banker, contemptuously. "It looks rather odd, though! Stop! maybe it's a wager. I've heard of gentlemen doing queer things for wagers. Or, maybe, he's cracked! Well, she's a nice girl; and hanging up this thing can't do any harm. I'll make inquiries about them, though, for all that."

Frowning portentously as he uttered this last cautious resolve, Mr. Dunball leisurely returned to the chemist's shop. He was, however, nothing like so ill-natured a man as he imigined himself to be; and, in spite of his dignity and his suspicions, he smiled far more cordially than he at all intended, as he now addressed little Annie Wray.

"It's out of our line, miss," said he; "but we'll hang the thing up to oblige you. Of course, if I want a reference, you can give it? Yes, yes! of course. There! there's the card in the window for you—a nice prominent place (look at it as you go out)—just between the string ot corn-plasters and the dried poppy-heads! I wish Mr. Wray success; though I rather think Tidbury is not quite the sort of place to come to for what you call elocution—eh?"

"Thank you, sir; and good morning," said little Annie. And she left the shop just as composedly as she had entered it.

"Cool little girl, that!" said Mr.Dunball, watching her progress down the street to No. 12.

"Pretty little girl, too!" thought the assistant, trying to watch, like his master, from the window.

"I should like to know who Mr. Wray is," said Mr. Dunball, turning back into the shop, as Annie disappeared. "And I'd give something to find out what Mr. Wray keeps in his cash-box," continued the banker-chemist, as he thoughtfully re-entered the mahogany money-chest in the back premises.

You are a wise man, Mr. Dunball; but you won't solve those two mysteries in a hurry, sitting alone in that Branch Bank sentry-box of yours! Can anybody solve them? I can.

Who is Mr. Wray? and what has he got in his cash-box? Come to No. 12 and see!

CHAPTER II.

MR. WRAY AND THE BRITISH DRAMA.

Before we go boldly into Mr. Wray's lodgings, I must speak a word or two about him, behind his back—but by no means slanderously. I will take his advertisement, now hanging up in the shop window of Messrs, Dunball and Dark, as the text of my discourse.

Mr. Reuben Wray became, as he phrased it, a "pupil of the late celebrated John Kemble, Esquire," in this manner: He began life by being apprenticed for three years to a statuary. Whether the occupation of taking casts and clipping stones proved of too sedentary a nature to suit his temperament, or whether an evil counsellor within him, whose name was vanity, whispered: "Seek public admiration, and be certain of public applause," I know not; but the fact is, that, as soon as his time was out, he left his master and his native place to join a band of strolling players; or, as he himself more magniloquently expressed it, he went on the stage.

Nature had gifted him with good lungs, large eyes, and a hook nose; his success before barn audiences was consequently brilliant. His professional exertions, it must be owned, barely sufficed to feed and clothe him; but then he had a triumph on the London stage, always present in the far perspective, to console him. While waiting this desirable event, he indulged himself in a little intermediate luxury, much in favor as a profitable resource for young men in extreme difficulties—he married; married at the age of nineteen, or thereabouts, the charming Columbine of the company.

And he got a good wife. Many people, I know, will refuse to believe this—it is a truth, nevertheless. The one redeeming success of the vast social failure which his whole existence was doomed to represent, was this very marriage of his with a strolling Columbine. She, poor girl, toiled as hard and as cheerfully to get her own bread after marriage, as before; trudged many a weary mile by his side from town to town, and never uttered a complaint; praised his acting; partook his hopes; patched his clothes; pardoned his ill-humor; paid court for him to his manager; made up his squabbles— in a word, and in the best and highest sense of that word, loved him. May I be allowed to add, that she only brought him one child—a girl? And, considering the state of his pecuniary resources, am I justified in ranking this circumstance as a strong additional proof of her excellent qualities as a married woman?

After much perseverance and many disappointments, Reuben at last succeeded in attaching himself to a regular provincial company— Tate Wilkinson's at York. He had to descend low enough from his original dramatic pedestal, before he succeeded in subduing the manager. From the leading business in tragedy and melo-drama, he sank at once, in the established provincial company, to a "minor utility"—words of theatrical slang signifying an actor who is put to the smaller dramatic uses which the necessities of the stage require. Still, in spite of this, he persisted in hoping for the chance that was never to come; and still poor Columbine faithfully hoped with him to the last.

Time passed—years of it; and this chance never arrived; and he and Columbine found themselves one day in London, forlorn and starving. Their life at this period would make a romance of itself, if I had time and space to write it; but I must get on as fast as may be, to later dates; and the reader must be contented merely to know that, at the last gasp—the last of hope; almost the last of life—Reuben got employment, as an actor of the lower degree, at Drury Lane.

Behold him, then, now—still a young man, but crushed in his young man's ambition forever—receiving the lowest theatrical wages for the lowest theatrical work; appearing on the stage as soldier, waiter, footman, and so on; with not a line in the play to speak; just showing his poverty-shrunken carcase to the audience, clothed in the frowsiest habiliments of the old Drury Lane wardrobe, for a minute or two at a time, at something like a shilling a night—a miserable being, in a miserable world; the world behind the scenes!

John Philip Kemble is now acting at the theatre; and his fame is rising to its climax. How the roar of applause follows him almost every time he leaves the scene! How majestically he stalks away into the green room, abstractedly inhaling his huge pinches of snuff as he goes! How the poor inferior brethren of the buskin, as they stand at the wing and stare upon him reverently, long for his notice; and how few of them can possibly get it! There is, nevertheless, one among this tribe of unfortunates whom he has really remarked, though he has not yet spoken to him. He has detected this man, shabby and solitary, constantly studying his acting from any vantage-ground the poor wretch could get amid the dust, dirt, draughts, and confusion behind the scenes. Mr. Kemble also observes, that whenever a play of Shakspeare's is being acted, this stranger has a tattered old book in his hands; and appears to be following the performance closely from the text, instead of huddling into warm corners over a pint of small beer, with the rest of his supernumerary brethren. Remarking these things, Mr. Kemble over and over again intends to speak to the man, and find out who he is; and over and over again utterly forgets it. But, at last; a day comes when the long-deferred personal communication really takes place; and it happens thus:

A new tragedy is to be produced—a pre-eminently bad one, by-the-by, even in those days of pre-eminently bad tragedy-writing. The scene is laid in Scotland; and Mr. Kemble is determined to play his part in a Highland dress. The idea of acting a drama in the appropriate costume of the period which that drama illustrates, is considered so dangerous an innovation that no one else dare follow his example; and he, of all the characters, is actually about to wear the only Highland dress in a Highland play.*This does not at all daunt him. He has acted Othello a night or two before, in the uniform of a British general officer,**and is so conscious of the enormous absurdity of the thing, that he is determined to persevere, and start the reform in stage costume, which he was afterwards destined so thoroughly to carry out.

* A fact! See Boaden's Life of Kemble, vol. i., p. 326.

** Another fact!! See the same work, vol. I, p. 256.

The night comes; the play begins. Just as the stage waits for Mr. Kemble, Mr. Kemble discovers that his goat-skin purse—one of the most striking peculiarities of the Highland dress—is not on him. There is no time to seek it—all is lost for the cause of costume! he must go on the stage exposed to public view as only half a Highlander! No! Not yet! While everybody else hurries frantically hither and thither in vain, one man quickly straps something about Mr. Kemble's waist, just in the nick of time. It is the lost purse! and Roscious after all steps on the stage, a Highlander complete from top to toe! On his first exit, Mr. Kemble inquires for the man who found the purse. It is that very poor player whom he has already remarked. The great actor had actually been carrying the purse about in his own hands before the performance; and, in a moment of abstraction, had put it down on a chair, in a dark place behind the prompter's box. The humble admirer, noticing everything he did, noticed this; and so found the missing goat-skin in time, when nobody else could.

"Sir, I am infinitely obliged to you," says Mr. Kemble, courteously, to the confused, blushing man before him. "You have saved me from appearing incomplete, and therefore ridiculous, before a Drury Lane audience. I have marked you, sir, before; reading, while waiting for your call, our divine Shakspeare—the poetic bond that unites all men, however professional distances may separate them. Accept, sir, this offered pinch—this pinch of snuff."

When the penniless player went home that night, what wonderful news he had for his wife! And how proud and happy poor Columbine was, when she heard that Reuben Wray had been offered a pinch of snuff out of Mr. Kemble's own box!

But the kind-hearted tragedian did not stop merely at a fine speech and a social condescension. Reuben read Shakspeare, when none of his comrades would have cared to look into the book at all; and that of itself was enough to make him interesting to Mr. Kemble. Besides, he was a young man; and might have capacities which only wanted encouragement. "I beg you to recite to me, sir," said the great John Philip, one night; desirous of seeing what his humble admirer really could do. The result of the recitation was unequivocal; poor Wray could do nothing that hundreds of his brethren could not have equalled. In him, the yearning to become a great actor was only the ambition without the power.

Still, Reuben gained something by the goat-skin purse. A timely word from his new protector raised him two or three degrees higher in the company, and increased his salary in proportion. He got parts now with some lines to speak in them; and condescension on condescension! Mr. Kemble actually declaimed them for his instruction at rehearsal, and solemnly showed him (oftener, I am afraid, in jest than in earnest) how a patriotic Roman soldier, or a bereaved father's faithful footman should tread the stage.

These instructions were always received by the grateful Wray in the most perfect good faith; and it was precisely in virtue of his lessons thus derived—numbering about half-a-dozen, and lasting about two minutes each—that he afterwards advertised himself, as teacher of elocution and pupil of John Kemble. Many a great man has blazed away famously before the public eye, as pupil of some other great man, from no larger a supply of original educational fuel than belonged to Mr. Reuben Wray.

Having fairly traced our friend to his connexion with Mr. Kemble, I may dismiss the rest of his advertisement more briefly. All, I suppose, that you now want further explained, is: How he came to teach elocution, and how he got on by teaching it.

Well: Reuben stuck fast to Drury Lane Theatre through rivalries, and quarrels, and disasters, and fluctuations in public taste, which overthrew more important interests than his own. The theatre was rebuilt, and burnt, and rebuilt again; and still old Wray (as he now began to be called) was part and parcel of the establishment, however, others might desert it. During this long lapse of monotonous years, affliction and death preyed cruelly on the poor actor's home. First, his kind, patient Columbine died; then, after a long interval, Columbine's only child married early; and woe is me! married a sad rascal, who first ill-treated and then deserted her. She soon followed her mother to the grave, leaving one girl—the little

Annie of this story—to Reuben's care. One of the first things her grand-father taught the child was to call herself Annie Wray. He never could endure hearing her dissolute father's name pronounced by anybody; and was resolved that she should always bear his own.

Ah! what woeful times were those for the poor player! How many a night he sat in the darkest corner behind the scenes, with his tattered Shakspeare—the only thing about him he had never pawned—in his hand, and the tears rolling down his hollow, painted cheeks, as he thought on the dear lost Columbine, and Columbine's child! How often those tears still stood thick in his eyes when he marched across the stage at the head of a mock army, or hobbled up to deliver the one eternal letter to the one eternal dandy hero of high comedy! Comedy, indeed! If the people before the lamps, who were roaring with laughter at the fun of the mercurial fine gentleman of the play, had only seen what was tugging at the heart of the miserable old stage footman who brought him his chocolate and newspapers, all the wit in the world would not have saved the comedy from being went over as the most affecting tragedy that was ever written.

But the time was to come—long after this, however—when Reuben's connexion with the theatre was to cease. As if fate had ironically bound up together the stage-destinies of the great actor and the small, the year of Mr. Kemble's retirement from the boards, was the year of Mr. Wray's dismissal from them.

He had been, for some time past, getting too old to be useful—then, the theatrical world in which he had been bred was altering, and he could not alter with it. A litle man with fiery black eyes, whose name was Edmund Kean, had come up from the country and blazed like a comet through the thick old conventional mists of the English stage. From that time, the new school began to rise, and the old old school to sink; and Reuben went down, with other insignificant atoms, in the vortex. At the end of the season, he was informed that his services were no longer required.

It was then, when he found himself once more forlorn in the world—almost as forlorn as when he had first come to London with poor

Columbine—that the notion of trying elocution struck him. He had a little sum of money to begin with, subscribed for him by his richer brethren when he left the theatre. Why might he not get on as a teacher of elocution in the country, just as some of his superior fellow-players got on in the same vocation in London? Necessity whispered, doubt not, but try. He had a grand-child to support—so he did try.

His method of teaching was exceedingly simple. He had one remedy for the deficiencies of every class whom he addressed—the Kemble remedy; he had watched Mr. Kemble year by year, till he knew every inch of him, and, so to speak, had learnt him by heart. Did a pupil want to walk the stage properly? teach him Mr. Kemble's walk. Did a rising politician want to become impresaive as an orator? teach him Mr. Kemble's gesticulations in Brutus. So, again, with regard to strictly vocal necessities. Did gentleman number one wish to learn the art of reading aloud? let him learn the Kemble cadences. Did gentleman number two feel weak in his pronunciation? let him sound vowels, consonants and crack-jaw syllables, just as Mr. Kemble sounded them on the stage. And out of what book were they to be taught? from what manual were the clergymen and orators, the aspirants for dramatic fame, the young ladies whose delivery was ungraceful, and the young gentlemen whose diction was improper, to be all alike improved? From Shakspeare—every one of them from Shakespeare! He had no idea of anything else; literature meant Shakspeare to *him*. It was his great glory and triumph, that he had Shakspeare by heart. All that he knew, every tender and loveable recollection, every small honor he had gained in his own poor blank sphere, was somehow sure to be associated with William Shakspeare!

And why not? What is Shakspeare but a great sun that shines upon humanity—the large heads and the little, alike? Have not the rays of that mighty light penetrated into many poor and lowly places for good? What marvel, then, that they should fall, pleasant and invigorating, even upon Reuben Wray? So, right or wrong, with Shakspeare for his text book, and Mr. Kemble for his model, our friend in his old age bravely invaded provincial England as a teacher of elocution, with all its supplementary accomplishments. And, wonderful to relate, though occasionally enduring dreadful privations, he just managed to make elocution—or what passed instead of it with his patrons—keep his grandchild and himself!

I cannot say that any orators or clergymen anxiously demanded secret improvement from him (see advertisement) at three and six-pence an hour; or that young ladies sought the graces of delivery, and young gentlemen the proprieties of diction (see advertisement again) from his experienced tongue. But he got on in other ways, nevertheless. Sometimes he was hired to drill the boys on a speech-day at a country-school. Sometimes he was engaged to prevent provincial amateur actors from murdering the dialogue outright, and incessantly jostling each other on the stage. In this last capacity, he occasionally got good employment, especially with regular amateur societies, who found his terms cheap enough, and his knowledge of theatrical discipline inestimably useful.

But chances like these were as nothing to the chances he got when he was occasionally employed to superintend all the toilsome part of the business, in arranging private theatricals at country houses. Here, he met with greater generosity than he had ever dared to expect; here, the letter from Mr. Kemble, vouching for his honesty and general stage-knowledge—the great actor's last legacy of kindness to him, which he carried about everywhere—was sure to produce prodigious effect. He and little Annie, and a third member of the family whom I shall hereafter introduce, lived for months together on the proceeds of such a windfall as a private theatrical party—for the young people, in the midst of their amusement, found leisure to pity the poor old ex-player, and to admire his pretty grand-daughter; and liberally paid him for his services full five times as much as he would ever have ventured to ask.

Thus, wandering about from town to town, sometimes miserably unsuccessful, sometimes re-animated by a little prosperity, he had come from Stratford-upon-Avon, while the present century was some twenty-five years younger than it is now, to try his luck at elocution with the people of Tidbury-on-the Marsh—to teach the graces of delivery at seventy years of age, with half his teeth gone! Will he succeed? I, for one, hope so. There is something in the spectacle of this poor old man, sorely battered by the world, yet still struggling for life, and for the grand-child whom he loved better than life—struggling hard, himself a remnant of a by-gone age, to keep up with a new age which has already got past him, and will hardly hear his feeble voice of other times, except to laugh at it— there is surely something in this which forbids all thought of ridicule, and bids fair with every body for compassion and good-will.

But we have had talk enough, by this time, about Mr. Reuben Wray. Let us now go at once and make acquaintance with him—not forgetting his mysterious cash-box—at No. 12.

CHAPTER III.

MR. WRAY AND HIS FAMILY.

The breakfast things are laid in the little drawing-room at Reuben's lodgings. This drawing-room, observe, has not been hired by our friend; he never possessed such a domestie luxury in his life. The apartment, not being taken, has only been lent to him by his landlady, who is hugely impressed by the tragic suavity of her, new tenant's manner and "delivery." The breakfast-things, I say again, are laid. Three cups, a loaf, half-a-pound of salt butter, some moist sugar in a saucer, and a black earthenware tea-pot, with a broken spout; such are the sumptuous preparations which tempt Mr. Wray and his family to come down at nine o'clock in the morning, and yet nobody appears!

Hark! there is a sound of creaking boots, descending, apparently, from some loft at the top of the house, so distant is the noise they make at first. This sound, coming heavily nearer and nearer, only stops at the drawing-room door, and heralds the entry of—Mr. Wray, of course? No! no such luck; my belief is, that we shall never succeed in getting to Mr. Wray personally. The individual in question is not even any relation of his; but he is a member of the family, for all that; and as the first to come down stairs, he certainly merits the reward of immediate notice.

He is nearly six feet high, proportionately strong and stout, and looks about thirty years of age. His gait is as awkward as it well can be; his features are large and ill-proportioned, his face is pitted with the small-pox, and what hair he has on his head—not much—seems to be growing in all sorts of contrary directions at once. I know nothing about him, personally, that I can praise, but his expression, and that is so thoroughly good-humored, so candid, so innocent even, that it really makes amends for everything else. Honesty and kindliness look out so brightly from his eyes, as to dazzle your observation of his clumsy nose, and lumpy mouth and chin, until you hardly know whether they are ugly or not. Some men, in a certain sense, are ugly with the lineaments of the Apollo Belvidere; and others handsome, with features that might sit for a caricature. Our new acquaintance was of the latter order. Allow me to introduce him to you: THE GENTLE READER—JULIUS CÆSAR. Stop! start not at those classic syllables; I will explain all.

The history of Mr. Martin Blunt, *alias* "Julius Cæsar," is a good deal like the history of Mr. Reuben Wray. Like him, Blunt began life with strolling players—not, however, as an actor, but as stage-carpenter, candle-snuffer, door-keeper, and general errand boy. On one occasion, when the company were ambitiously bent on the horrible profanation of performing Shakspeare's Julius Cæsar, the actor who was to personate the emperor fell ill. Nobody was left to supply his place—every other available member of the company was engaged in the play; so, in despair, they resorted to Martin Blunt. He was big enough for a Roman hero; and that was all they looked to.

They first cut out as much of his part as they could, and then half crammed the rest into his reluctant brains; they clapped a white sheet about the poor lad's body for a toga, stuck a truncheon into his hand, and a short beard on his chin; and remorselessly pushed him on the stage. His performance was received with shouts of laughter; he went through it; was duly assassinated; and fell with a thump that shook the surrounding scenery to its centre, and got him a complete round of applause all to himself.

He never forgot this. It was his first and last appearance; and, in the innocence of his heart, he boasted of it on every occasion, as the great distinction of his life. When he found his way to London, and as a really skillful carpenter, procured employment at Drury Lane, his fellow workmen managed to get the story of his first performance out of him directly, and made a standing joke of it. He was elected a general butt, and nick-named "Julius Cæsar," by universal acclamation. Everybody conferred on, him that classic title; and I only follow the general fashion in these pages. If you don't like the name, call him any other you please; he is too good-humored to be offended with you, do what you will. He was thus introduced to old Wray:

The Stolen Mask; or, The Mysterious Cash-Box

At the time when Reuben was closing his career at Drury Lane, our stout young carpenter had just begun to work there. One night, about a week before the performance of a new pantomime, some of the heavy machinery tottered just as Wray was passing by it; and would have fallen on him, but for "Julius Cæsar," (I really can't call him Blunt!) who, at the risk of his own limbs, caught the tumbling mass, and by a tremendous exertion of main strength, arrested it in its fall, till the old man had hobbled out of harm's way. This led to gratitude friendship, intimacy. Wray and his preserver, in spite of the difference in their characters and ages, seemed to suit each other, somehow. In fine, when Reuben started to teach elocution in the country, the carpenter followed him, as protector, assistant, servant, or whatever you please.

"Julius Cæsar" had one special motive for attaching himself to old Wray's fortunes, which will speedily appear, when little Annie enters the drawing-room. Awkward as he might be, he was certainly no encumbrance. He made himself useful and profitable in fifty different ways. He took round hand bills soliciting patronage; constructed the scenery when Mr. Wray got private theatrical engagements: worked as journeyman carpenter when other resources failed, and was, in fact, ready for anything, from dunning for a bad debt, to cleaning a pair of shoes. His master might at times be as fretful as he pleased, and treat him like an infant during occasional fits af crossness—he never replied, and never looked sulky. The only things he could not be got to do were to abstain from inadvertently knocking everything down that came in his reach, and to improve the action of his arms and legs on the principle of the late Mr. Kemble.

Let us return to the drawing-room and the breakfast things. "Julius Cæsar," of the creaking boots, came into the room with a small work-box (which he had been secretly engaged in making for some time past) in one hand, and a new muslin cravat in the other. It was Annie's birth-day. The box was a present; the cravat, what the French would call, a homage to the occasion.

His first proceeding was to drop the work-box and pick it up again in a great hurry; his second, to go to the looking-glass, (no such piece of furniture ornamented his loft bed-room,) and try to put on the new cravat. He had only half tied it, and was hesitating, utterly helpless, over the bow, when a light step sounded on the floor-cloth outside. Annie came in.

"Julius Cæsar at the looking-glass! Oh, good gracious, what *can* have come to him!" exclaimed the little girl, with a merry laugh.

How fresh, and blooming, and pretty she looked, as she ran up the next moment; and telling him to stop, tied his cravat directly—standing on tip-toe. "There," she cried, "now that's done, what have you got to say to me, sir, on my birth-day?"

"I've got a box, and I'm so glad it's your birthday," says Julius Cæsar, too confused by the suddenness of the cravat-tying to know exactly what he is talking about.

"Oh, what a splendid work-box! how kind of you, to be sure! what care I shall take of it! Come, sir, I suppose I must tell you to give me a kiss after that," and, standing on tip-toe again, she held up her fresh, rosy cheek to be kissed, with such a pretty mixture of bashfulness, gratitude and arch enjoyment in her look, that "Julius Cæsar," I regret to say, felt inclined then and there to go down upon both his knees and worship her outright.

Before the decorous reader has time to consider all this very improper, I had better, perhaps, interpose a word, and explain that Annie Wray had promised Martin Blunt, (I give his real name again here, because this is serious business,) yes—had actually promised him that one day she would be his wife. She kept all her promises; but I can tell you she was especially determined to keep this.

Impossible! exclaims the lady reader. With her good looks, she might aspire many degrees above a poor carpenter; besides, how could she possibly care about a great lumpish, awkward fellow, who *is* ugly, say what you will about his expression?

I might reply, madam, that our little Annie had looked rather deeper than the skin in choosing her husband; and had found out certain qualities of heart and disposition about this poor carpenter, which made her love—aye, and respect and admire him, too. But I prefer asking you a question, by way of answer. Did you never meet with any individuals of your own sex, lovely, romantic, magnificent young women, who have fairly stupefied the whole circle of their relatives and friends by marrying particularly short, scrubby, matter-of-fact, middle-aged men, showing, too, every symptom of fondness for them into the bargain? I fancy you must have seen such cases as I have mentioned; and when you can explain them to *my* satisfaction, I shall be happy to explain the anomalous engagement of little Annie to *yours*.

In the meantime, it may be well to relate that this odd love affair was only once hinted at to Mr. Wray. The old man flew into a frantic passion directly, and threatened dire extremities if the thing was ever thought of more. Lonely and bereaved of all other ties, as he was, he had, in regard to his grand-daughter, that jealousy of other people loving her, which is of all weaknesses, in such cases as his, the most pardonable and the most pure. If a duke had asked for Annie in marriage, I doubt very much whether Mr. Wray would have let him have her, except upon the understanding that they were all to live together.

Under these circumstances, the engagement was never hinted at again. Annie told her lover they must wait, and be patient, and remain as brother and sister to one another, till better chances and better times came. And "Julius Cæsar" listened, and strictly obeyed. He was a good deal like a large, faithful dog to his little betrothed; he loved her, watched over her, guarded her, with his whole heart and strength; only asking in return the privilege of fulfilling her slightest wish.

Well; this kiss, about which I have been digressing so long, was fortunately just over, when another footstep sounded outside; the door opened; and—yes! we have got him at last, in his own proper person! Enter Mr. Reuben Wray!

Age has given him a stoop, which he tries to conceal, but cannot. His cheeks are hollow; his face is seamed with wrinkles, the work not only of time, but of trial, too. Still, there is vitality of mind, courage of heart, about the old man, even yet. His look has not lost all its animation, nor his smile its warmth. *There* is the true Kemble walk, and the true Kemble carriage for you, if you like! *there* is the second hand tragic grandeur and propriety, which the unfortunate Julius Cæsar daily contemplates, yet cannot even faintly copy! Look at his dress again. Thread-bare as it is, (patched, I am afraid, in some places,) there is not a speck of dust on it, and what little hair is left on his bald head is as carefully brushed as if he rejoiced in the love-locks of Absalom himself. No! though misfortune, and disappointment, and grief, and heavy-handed penury have all been assailing him ruthlessly enough for more than half a century, they have not got the old fellow down yet! At seventy years of age, he is still on his legs in the prize-ring of life; badly punished all over, (as the pugilists say,) but determined to win the fight to the last!

"Many happy returns of the day, my love," says old Reuben, going up to Annie, and kissing her. "This is the twentieth birth-day of yours I've lived to see. Thank God for that!"

"Look at my present, grand-father," cries the little girl, proudly showing her work-box. "Can you guess who made it?"

"You are a good fellow, Julius Cæsar!" exclaims Mr. Wray, guessing directly. "Good morning; shake hands." (Then, in a lower voice, to Annie,) "Has he broken anything in particular since he's been up?" "No!" "I'm very glad to hear it. Julius Cæsar, let me offer you a pinch of snuff," and here he pulled out his box quite in the Kemble style. He had his natural manner and his Kemble manner. The first only appeared when anything greatly pleased or affected him—the second was for those ordinary occasions when he had time to remember that he was a teacher of elocution and a pupil of the English Roscius.

"Thank ye, kindly, sir," said the gratified carpenter, cautiously advancing his huge finger and thumb towards the offered box.

"Stop!" cried old. Wray, suddenly withdrawing it. He always lectured to Julius Cæsar on elocution when he had nobody else to teach, just to keep his hand in. "Stop! that won't do. In the first place, 'Thank ye, kindly, sir,' though good humored, is grossly inelegant. 'Sir, I am obliged to you,' is the proper phrase—mind you sound the *i* in obliged—never say *obleeged,* as some people do; and remember, what I am now telling *you,* Mr. Kemble once said to the Prince Regent! The next hint I have to give you is this—never take your pinch of snuff with your right hand finger and thumb; it should be always the left. Perhaps you would like to know why?"

"Yes, please, sir," says the admiring disciple, very humbly.

" 'Yes, *if* you please, sir,' would have been better; but let that pass as a small error. And now I will tell you why, in an anecdote. Matthews was one day mimicking Mr. Kemble to his face, in Penruddock—the great scene where he stops to take a pinch of snuff. 'Very good, Matthews; very like me,' says Mr. Kemble, complacently, when Matthews had done; 'but you have made one great mistake.' 'What's that?' cries Matthews, sharply. 'My friend, you have not represented me taking snuff like a gentleman; now, I always do. You took your pinch, in imitating my Penruddock, with your right hand; I use my *left*—a gentleman invariably does, because then he has his right hand always clean from tobacco to give to his friend!' There! remember that; and now you may take your pinch."

Mr. Wray next turned round to speak to Annie; but his voice was instantly drowned in a perfect explosion of sneezes, absolutely screamed out by the unhappy "Julius Cæsar," whose nasal nerves were convulsed by the snuff. Mentally determining never to offer his box to his faithful follower again, old Reuben gave up making his proposed remark, until they were all quietly seated round the breakfast table; then he returned to the charge with renewed determination.

"Annie, my dear," said he, "you and I have read a great deal together of our divine Shakspeare, as Mr. Kemble always called him. You are my regular pupil, you know, and ought to be able to quote by this time almost as much as I can. I am going to try you with something new—suppose I had offered *you* the pinch of snuff, (Mr. Julius Cæsar shall never have another, I can promise him,) what would you have said from Shakspeare applicable to *that?* Just think now!"

"But, grand-father, snuff wasn't invented in Shakspeare's time—was it?" said Annie.

"That's of no consequence," retorted the old man; "Shakspeare was for *all* time; you can quote him for everything in the world, as long as the world lasts. Can't you quote him for snuff? I can, Now, listen. You say to me, 'I offer you a pinch of snuff?' I answer from Cymbeline (Act iv., scene 2:) 'Pisiano! I'll now taste of thy drug.' There! won't that do? What's snuff but a drug for the nose? It just fits—everything of the divine Shakspeare does; when you know him by heart, as I do—eh, little Annie? And now give me some more sugar; I wish it was lump for your sake, dear; but I'm afraid we can only afford moist. Anybody called about the advertisement? a new pupil this morning—eh?"

No! no pupils at all; not a man, woman, or child in the town, to teach elocution to yet! Mr, Wray was not at all despondent about this; he had made up his mind that a pupil must come in the course of the day; and that was enough for him. His little quibbling from Shakspeare about the snuff had put him in the best of good humors, He went on making quotations, talking elocution, and eating bread and butter, as brisk and happy, as if all Tidbury had combined to form one mighty class for him, and resolved to pay ready money for every lesson.

But after breakfast, when the things were taken away, the old man seemed suddenly to recollect something which changed his manner altogether. He grew first embarrassed; then silent; then pulled out his Shakspeare, and began to read with ostentatious assiduity, as if he were especially desirous that nobody should speak to him.

At the same time, a close observer might have detected Mr. "Julius Cæsar" making varous uncouth signs and grimaces to Annie, which the little girl apparently understood, but did not know how to answer. At last, with an effort, as if she were summoning extraordinary resolution, she said:

"Grand-father—you have not forgotten your promise?"

No answer from Mr. Wray. Probably, he was too much absorbed over Shakspeare to hear.

"Grand-father," repeated Annie, in a louder tone; "you promised to explain a certain mystery to us, on my birth-day."

Mr. Wray was obliged to hear this time. He looked up with a very perplexed face.

"Yes, dear," said he; "I did promise; but I almost wish I had not. It's rather a dangerous mystery to explain, little Annie, I can tell you! Why should you be so very curious to know about it?"

"I'm sure, grand-father," pleaded Annie, "you can't say I am over-curious, or Julius Cæsar either, in wanting to know about it. Just recollect—we had been only three days at Stratford-upon-Avon, when you came in, looking so dreadfully frightened, and said we must go away directly. And you made us pack up; and we all went off in a hurry, more like prisoners escaping, than honest people."

"We did!" groaned old Reuben, beginning to look like a culprit already.

"Well," continued Annie; and you wouldn't tell us a word of what is was all for, beg as hard as we might. And then, when we asked why you never let that old cash-box (which I used to keep my odds and ends in) out of your own hands, after we left Stratford—you wouldn't tell us that, either, and ordered us never to mention the thing again. It was only in one of your particular good humors, that I just got you to promise you would tell us all about it on my next birth-day—to celebrate the day, you said. I'm sure we are to be trusted with any secrets; and I don't think it's being very curious to want to know this."

"Very well!" said Mr. Wray, rising, with a sort of desperate calmness; "I've promised, and, come what may, I'll keep my promise. Wait here; I'll be back directly." And he left the room, in a great hurry.

He returned immediately, with the cash-box. A very battered, shabby affair, to make such a mystery about! thought Annie, as he put the box on the table, and solemnly laid his hands across it.

"Now, then," said old Wray, in his deepest tragedy-tones, and with very serious looks; "promise me, on your word of honor—both of you—that you'll never say a word of what I'm going to tell, to anybody, on any account whatever—I don't care what happens—*on any account whatever!*"

Annie and her lover gave their promises directly, and very seriously. They were getting a little agitated by all these elaborate preparations for the coming disclosure.

"Shut the door!" said Mr. Wray, in a stage whisper. "Now sit close and listen; I'm ready to explain the mystery."

CHAPTER IV.

MYSTERIES OF THE CASH-BOX.

"I suppose," said old Reuben, "you have neither of you forgotten that, on the second day of our visit to Stratford, I went out in the afternnon to dine with an intimate friend of mine, whom I'd known from a boy, and who lived at some little distance from the town—"

"Forget that!" cried Annie; "I don't think we ever shall—I was frightened about you, all the time you were gone."

"Frightened about what?" asked Mr. Wray, sharply. "Do you mean to tell me, Annie, you suspected"—

"I don't know what I suspected, grand-father; but I thought your going away by yourself, to sleep at your friend's house, (as you told us,) and not to come back till the next morning, something very extraordinary. I was the first time we had ever slept under different roofs—only think of that!"

"I'm ashamed to say, my dear"—rejoined Mr. Wray, suddenly beginning to look and speak very uneasily—"that I turned hypocrite, and something worse, too, on that occasion. I deceived you. I had no friend to go and dine with; and didn't pass that night in any house at all."

"Grand-father!" cried Annie, jumping up in a fright, "what can you mean!"

"Beg pardon, sir," added "Julius Cæsar," turning very red, and slowly clenching both his enormous fists as he spoke—"Beg pardon; but if you was put upon, or made fun of by any chaps that night, I wish you'd just please to tell me where I could find 'em."

"Nobody ill-used me," said the old man, in steady, and even solemn tones. "I passed that night by the grave of William Shakspeare, in Stratford-upon-Avon Church!"

Annie sank back into her seat and lost all her pretty complexion in a moment. The worthy carpenter gave such a start, that he broke the back rail of his chair. It was a variation on his usual performances of this sort, which were generally confined to cups, saucers, and wine-glasses.

Mr. Wray took no notice of the accident. This was of itself enough to show that he was strongly agitated by something. After a momentary silence, he spoke again, completely forgetting the Kemble manner and the Kemble elocution as he went on.

"I say again, I passed all that night in Stratford Church; and you shall know for what. You went with me, Annie, in the morning—it was Tuesday; yes, Tuesday morning—to see Shakespeare's bust in the church. You looked at it, like other people, just as a curiosity—I looked at it, as the greatest treasure in the world; the only true likeness of Shakespeare! It's been done from a mask, taken from his own face, after death—I know it; I don't care what people say, I know it. Well, when we went home, I felt as if I'd seen Shakspeare himself, risen from the dead! Strangers would laugh if I told them so; but it's true—I did feel it. And this thought came across me, quick, like the shooting of a sudden pain; I must make that face of Shakespeare mine; my possession, my companion, my great treasure that no money can pay for! And I've got it! Here! the only cast from the Stratford bust is locked up in this old cash-box!"

He paused a moment. Astonishment kept both his auditors silent.

"You both know," he continued, "that I was bred apprentice to a statuary. Among other things, he taught me to make casts; it was part of our business—the easiest part. I knew I could take a mould off the Stratford bust, if I had the courage; and the courage came to me; on the Tuesday, it came. I went and bought some plaster, some soft soap, and a quart basin—those were my materials—and tied them up together in an old canvass bag. Water was all I wanted besides; and that I saw in the church vestry, in the morning—a jug of it, left I suppose since Sunday, where it had been put for the clergyman's use. I could carry my bag under my cloak quite comfortably, you understand. The only thing that troubled me now was how to get into the church again, without being suspected. While I was thinking, I passed the inn door. Some people were on the steps, talking to some other people in the street; they were making an appointment to go all together, and see Shakespeare's bust and grave that very afternoon. This was enough for me; I determined to go into the church with them."

"What! and stop there all night, grand-father?"

"And stop there all night, Annie. Taking a mould, you know, is not a very long business; but I wanted to take mine unobserved; and the early morning; before anybody was up, was the only time to do that safely in the church. Besides, I wanted plenty of leisure, because I wasn't sure I should succeed at first, after being out of practice so long in making casts. But you shall hear how I did it, when the time comes. Well, I made up the story about dining and sleeping at my friend's, because I didn't know what might happen, and because— because, in short, I didn't like to tell you what I was going to do. So I went out secretly, near the church, and waited for the party coming. They were late—late in the afternoon, before they came. We all went in together; I with my bag, you know, hid under my cloak. The man who showed us over the church in the morning, luckily for me, wasn't there; an old woman took his duty for him in the afternoon. I waited till the visitors were all congregated round Shakspeare's grave, bothering the poor woman with foolish questions about him. I knew that was my time, and slipped off into the vestry, and opened the cupboard, and hid myself among the surplices, as quiet as a mouse. After awhile, I heard one of the strangers in the church (they were very rude, boisterous people) asking the other, what had become of the 'old fogy with the cloak?' and the other answered that the must have gone out, like a wise man, and that they had all better go after him, for it was precious cold and dull in the church. They went away, I heard the doors shut, and knew I was locked in for the night."

"All night in a church! Oh, grand-father, how frightened you must have been!"

"Well, Annie, I was a little frightened; but more at what I was going to do, than at being alone in the church. Let me get on with my story, though. Being autumn weather, it grew too dark after the people went, for me to do anything then; so I screwed my courage up to wait for the morning. The first thing I did was to go and look quietly, all by myself, at the bust; and I made up my mind that I could take the mould in about three or four pieces. All I wanted was what they call a mask; that means just a forehead and face, without the head. It's an easy thing to take a mask off a bust—I knew I could do it; but, somehow, I didn't feel quite comfortable just then. The bust began to look very awful to me, in the fading light, all alone in the church. It was almost like looking at the ghost of Shakspeare, in that place, and at that time. If the door hadn't been locked, I think I should have run out of the church; but I couldn't do that; so I knelt down and kissed the grave-stone—a curious fancy coming over me as I did so, that it was like wishing Shakspeare good night—and then I groped my way back to the vestry. When I got in, and had shut the door between me and the grave, I grew bolder, I can tell you; and thought to myself— I'm doing no harm; I'm not going to hurt the bust; I only want what an Englishman and an old actor may fairly covet, a copy of Shakspeare's face; why shouldn't I eat my bit of supper here, and say my prayers as usual, and get my nap into the bargain, if I can? Just as I thought that——BANG went the clock, striking the hour! It almost knocked me down, bold as I felt the moment before. I was obliged to wait till it was all still again, before I could pull the bit of bread and cheese I had got with me out of my pocket. And when I did, I couldn't eat; I was too impatient for the morning; so I sat down in the parson's arm-chair; and tried, next, whether I could sleep at all."

"And could you, grand-father?"

"No—I couldn't sleep either; at least, not at first. It was quite dark now; and I began to feel cold and awe-struck again. The only thing I could think of to keep up my spirits at all, was first saying my prayers, and then quoting Shakspeare. I went at it, Annie, like a dragon; play after play—except the tragedies; I was afraid of them, in a church at night, all by myself. Well, I think I had got half through the Mid-summer Night's Dream, whispering over bit after bit of it; when I whispered myself into a doze. Then I fell into a queer sleep; and then I had such a dream! I dreamt that the church was full of moonlight—brighter moonlight than ever I saw awake. I walked out of the vestry; and there were the fairies of the Mid-summer Night's Dream—all creatures like sparks of silver light—dancing round the Shakspeare bust! The moment they caught sight of me, they all called out in their sweet nightingale voices: 'Come along, Reuben! sly old Reuben! we know what you're here for, and we don't mind you a bit! You love Shakspeare, and so do we—dance, Reuben, and be happy! Shakspeare likes an old actor; he was an actor himself—nobody sees us! we're out for the night! foot it, old Reuben—foot it away!' And we all danced like mad; now, up in the air; now, down on the pavement; and now, all round the bust five hundred thousand times at least without stopping, till——BANG went the clock! and I woke up in the dark, in a cold perspiration."

"I'm in one too!" gasped "Julius Cæsar," dabbing his brow vehemently with a ragged cotton pocket handkerchief.

"Well, after that dream I fell to reciting again; and got another doze; and had another dream—a terrible one, about ghosts and witches, that I don't recollect so well as the other. I woke up once more, cold, and in a great fright that I'd slept away all the precious morning daylight. No! all dark still. I went into the church again, and then back to the vestry, not being able to stay there. I suppose I did this a dozen times without knowing why. At last, never going to sleep again, I got somehow through the night—the night that seemed never to be done. Soon after daybreak, I began to walk up and down the church briskly, to get myself warm, keeping at it for a long time. Then, just as I saw through the windows that the sun was rising, I opened my bag at last, and got ready for work. I can tell you my hand trembled and my sight grew dim—I think the tears were in my eyes; but I don't know why—as I soaped the stone all over to prevent the plaster I was going to put on it from sticking. Then I mixed up the plaster and water in my quart basin, taking care to leave no lumps, and finding it come as natural to me as if I had only left the statuary's shop yesterday; then—but it's no use telling you, little Annie, about what you don't understand. I'd better say shortly I made the mould, in four pieces, as I thought I should—two for the upper part of the face, and two for the lower. Then, having put on the outer plaster case to hold the mould, I pulled all off clean together, and looked, and knew that I had got a mask of Shakspeare from the Stratford bust!"

"Oh, grand-father, how glad you must have been then!"

"No, that was the odd part of it. At first, I felt as if I had robbed the bank, or the King's jewels, or had set fire to a train of gunpowder to blow up all London; it seemed such a thing to have done! Such a tremendously daring, desperate thing! But, a little while after, a frantic sort of joy came over me; I could hardly prevent myself from shouting and singing at the top of my voice. Then I felt a perfect fever of impatience to cast the mould directly, and see whether the mask would come out without a flaw. The keeping down that impatience was the hardest thing I had had to do since I first got into the church."

"But, please, sir, whenever did you get out at last? Do pray tell us that!" asked "Julius Cæsar."

"Not till after the clock had struck twelve, and I'd eaten all my bread and cheese," said Mr. Wray, rather piteously. "I was glad enough when I heard the church door open at last, from the vestry where I had popped in but a moment before. It was the same woman came in who had shown the bust in the afternoon. I waited my time, and then slipped into the church; but she turned round sharply, just as I'd got half way out and came up to me. I never was frightened by an old woman before; but I can tell you she frightened me. 'Oh! there you are again!' says she. 'Come, I say! this won't do. You sneaked out yesterday afternoon without paying anything; and you sneak in again after me, as soon as I open the door this morning—ain't you ashamed of being so shabby as that, at your age—ain't you?' I never paid money in my life, Annie, with pleasure, till I gave that old woman some to stop her mouth! And I don't recollect either that I'd ever tried to run since leaving the stage (where we had a good deal of running, first and last, in the battlescenes;) but I ran as soon as I got well away from the church, I can promise you—ran almost the whole way home."

"That's what made you look so tired when you came in, grand-father," said Annie; "we couldn't think what was the matter with you at the time."

"Well," continued the old man, "as soon as I could possibly get away from you after coming back, I went and locked myself into my bed-room, pulled the mould in a great hurry out of the canvass bag, and took the cast at once—a beautiful cast! a perfect cast! I never produced a better when I was in good practice, Annie. When I sat down on the side of the bed, and looked at Shakspeare—my Shakspeare—got with so much danger, and made with my own hands—so white and pure and beautiful, just out of the mould! Old as I am, it was all I could do to keep myself from dancing for joy."

"And yet, grand-father,' said Annie reproachfully, you could keep all that joy to yourself—you could keep it from me!"

"It was wrong, my love, wrong on my part not to trust you—I'm sorry for it now. But the joy, after all, lasted a very little while—only from the afternoon to the evening. In the evening, if you remember, I went out to the butcher's to buy something for my own supper; something I could fancy, to make me comfortable before I went to bed (you little thought how I wanted my bed that night.) Well, when I got into the shop, several people were there; and what do you think they were all talking about? It makes me shudder even to remember it now! They were talking about a cast having been taken—feloniously taken, just fancy that—from the Stratford bust!"

Annie looked pale again instantly at this part of the story. As for "Julius Cæsar," though he said nothing, he was evidently suffering from a second attack of the sympathetic cold perspiration which had already troubled him. He used the cotton handkerchief more copiously than ever just at this moment.

"The butcher was speaking when I came in," pursued Mr. Wray. " 'Who's been and took it,' says the fellow, (his grammar and elocution were awful, Annie!) 'nobody don't know yet; but the Town Council will know by to-morrow, and then he'll be took himself.' 'Ah,' says a dirty little man in black, 'he'll be cast into prison for taking a cast—eh?' They laughed, actually laughed at this vile pun. Then another man asked how this had been found out. 'Some says,' answered the butcher, 'he was seen a doin' of it through the window, by some chap looking in accidental like. Some says, nobody don't know but the church wardens, and they won't tell till they've got him.' 'Well,' says a woman, waiting with a basket to be served, 'but how will they get him?—(two chops, please, when you're quite ready)—that's the thing; how will they get him?' 'Quiet easy; take my word for it;' says the man who made the bad pun. 'In the first place, they've posted up hand-bills, offering a reward for him; in the second place, they're going to examine the people who show the church; in the third place—' 'Bother your places!' cried the woman, 'I wish I could get my chops.' 'There you are, Mum,' says the butcher, cutting off the chops, 'and if you want my opinion about this business, it's this here: they'll transport him right away, in no time.' 'They can't,' cries the dirty man, 'they can only imprison him.' 'For life—eh?' says the woman, going off with the chops. 'Be so kind as to let me have a couple of kidneys;' said I, for my knees knocked together, and I could stand it no longer."

"Then you thought, grand-father, that they suspected you?"

"I thought everything that was horrible, Annie. However, I got my kidneys, and went out unhindered, leaving them still talking about it. On my way home I saw the hand-bill—the hand-bill itself! Ten pounds reward for apprehending the man who had taken the cast! I read it twice through in a sort of trance of terror. My mask taken away, and myself put in prison, if not transported—that was the prospect I had to give me an appetite for the kidneys. There was only one thing to be done; to get away from Stratford while I had the chance. The night coach went that very evening straight through to this place, which was far enough off for safety. We had some money, you know left, after that last private theatrical party, where they treated us so generously. In short, I made you pack up, Annie, as you said just now, and got you both off by the coach, in time, not daring to speak a word about my secret, and as miserable as I could be the whole journey. But let us say no more about that—here we are, safe and sound; and here's my face of Shakspeare—my diamond above all price—safe and sound, too! You shall see it; you shall look at the mask, both of you, and then, I hope, you'll acknowledge that you know as much as I do about the mystery!"

"But, the mould," cried Annie; "haven't you got the mould with you, too?"

"Lord bless my soul!" exclaimed Mr. Wray, slapping both hands, in desperation, on the lid of the cash-box. "Between the fright and the hurry of getting away, I quite forgot it—it's left at Stratford!"

"Left at Stratford!" echoed Annie, with a vague feeling of dismay, that she could not account for.

"Yes; rolled up in the canvas bag, and poked behind the landlord's volumes of the '*Annual Register*,' on the top shelf of the cupboard, in my bed-room. Between thinking of how to take care of the mask, and how to take care of myself, I quite forgot it. Don't look so frightened, Annie! The people at the lodgings are not likely to find it; and if they did, they wouldn't know what it was, and would throw it away. I've got the mask; and that's all I want—the mould is of no consequence to me now—it's the mask that's everything—everything in the world!"

"I can't help feeling frightened, grand-father; and I can't help wishing you had brought away the mould, though I don't know why."

"You're frightened, Annie, about the Stratford people coming after me here—that's what you're frightened about. But, if you and Julius Cæsar keep the secret from everybody—and I know you will—there is no fear at all. They won't catch me back at Stratford again, or you either; and if the church wardens themselves found the mould, that wouldn't tell them where I was gene, would it? Look up, you silly little Annie! We're quite safe here. Look up, and see the great sight I'm going to show you—a sight that nobody in England can show but me—the mask—the mask of Shakspeare!"

His cheeks flushed, his fingers trembled, as he took a key out of his pocket and put it into the lock of the old cash-box. "Julius Cæsar," breathless with wonder and suspense, clapped both his hands behind him, to make sure of breaking nothing this time. Even Annie caught the infection of the old man's triumph and delight, and breathed quicker than usual when she heard the click of the opening lock.

"There!" cried Mr. Wray, throwing back the lid; there is the face of William Shakspeare! there is the treasure which the greatest lord in this land doesn't possess—a copy of the Stratford bust! Look at the forehead! Who's got such a forehead now? Look at his eyes; look at his nose. He was not only the greatest man that ever lived, but the handsomest, too! Who says this isn't just what his face was; his face taken after death? Who's bold enough to say so? Just look at the mouth, dropped and open—that's one proof. Look at the cheek, under the right eye; don't you see a little paralytic gathering up of the muscle, not visible on the other side—that's another proof. Oh, Annie, Annie! there's the very face that once looked out, alive and beaming, on this poor old world of ours! There's the man who's comforted me, informed me, made me what I am! There's the 'counterfeit presentment,' the precious earthly relic of that great, great spirit who is now with the angels in Heaven, and singing among the sweetest of them!"

His voice grew faint, and his eyes moistened. He stood looking on the mask, with a rapture and a triumph which no speech could express. At such moments as those, even through that poor, meagre face, the immortal spirit within could still shine out in the beauty which never dies—even in that frail old earthly tenement, could still vindicate outwardly the divine destiny of all mankind!

They were yet gathered silently round the Shakspeare cast, when a loud knock sounded at the room door. Instantly, old Reuben banged down the lid of the cash-box, and locked it; and as instantly, without waiting for permission to enter, a strangar walked in.

He was dressed in a long great-coat, wore a red comforter round his neck, and carried a very old and ill-looking cat-skin cap in his hand. His face was uncommonly dirty; his eyes uncommonly inquisitive; his whiskers uncommonly plentiful; and his voice most uncommonly and determinately gruff, in spite of his efforts to dulcify it for the occasion.

"Miss and gentlemen both, beggin' all your pardons," said this new arrival, "vich is Mr. Wray?" As he spoke, his eyes traveled all round the room, seeing everything and everybody in it; and then glancing sharply at the cash-box.

"I am Mr. Wray, sir," exclaimed our old friend, considerably startled, but recovering the Kemble manner and the Kemble elocution as if by magic.

"Wery good," said the stranger. "Then, beggin' your pardon again sir, in pertickler, could you be so kind as to 'blige me with a card o' terms? It's for a young gentleman as wants you, Mr. Wray," he continued in a whisper, approaching the old man, and quite abstractedly leaning one hand on the cash-box.

"Take your hand off that box, sir," cried Mr. Wray, in a very fierce manner, but with a very trembling voice. At the same moment, "Julius Cæsar" advanced a step or two, partially doubling his fist. The man with the cat-skin cap had probably never before been so nearly knocked down in his life. Perhaps he suspected as much, for he took his hand off the box in a great hurry.

"It was inadwertent, sir," he remarked in explanation—"a little inadwertency of mine, that's all. But could you 'blige me vith that card of terms? The young gentleman as wants it has heerd of your advertisement; and, bein' d'awful shaky in his pronunciashun, as vell as 'scruciatin' bad at readin' aloud, he's 'ard up for improvement—the sort of secret thing you gives, you know, to the oraytors and the clujjymen, at three and six an hour. You'll heer from him in secret, Mr. Wray, sir; and precious vork you'll 'ave to git him to rights; but do just 'blige mo vith the card o' terms and the number of the 'ouse; 'cos I promised to git 'em for him to-day."

"There is a card, sir, and I will engage to improve his delivery, be it ever so bad," said Mr. Wray, considerably relieved at hearing the real nature of the stranger's errand.

"Miss, and gentlemen both, good mornin'," said the man, putting on his cat-skin cap, "you'll heer from the young gentleman to-day; and wotever you do, sir, mind you keep the h'applicashun a secret— mind that!" He winked and went out.

"I declare," muttered Mr. Wray, as the door closed, "I thought he was a thief-taker from Stratford. Think of his being only a messenger from a new pupil!, I told you we should have a pupil today. I told you so."

"A very strange looking messenger, grand-father, for a young gentleman to choose!" said Annie.

"He can't help his looks, my dear; and I'm sure we shan't mind them, if he brings us money. Have you seen enough of the mask? if you haven't, I'll open the box again."

"Enough for to-day, I think, grand-father. But, tell me why you keep the mask in the old cash-box?"

"Because I've nothing else, Annie, that will hold it, and lock up, too. I was sorry, my dear, to disturb your 'odds and ends,' as you call them; but really there was nothing else to take. Stop, I've a thought!

Julius Cæsar shall make me a new box for the mask, and then you shall have your old one back again."

"I don't want it, grand-father! I'd rather we none of us had it. Carrying a cash-box like that about with us, might make some people think we had money in it."

"Money! People think I have any money! Come, come, Annie! that really won't do! That's much too good a joke, you sly little puss, you!" And the old man laughed heartily, as he hurried off, to deposit the precious mask in his bed-room.

"You'll make that new box, Julius Cæsar, won't you?" said Annie, earnestly, as soon as her grandfather left the room.

"I'll get some wood, this very day," answered the carpenter, "and turn out such a box, by tomorrow, as—as—" He was weak at comparisons; so he stopped at the second "as."

"Make it quick, dear, make it quick," said the little girl, anxiously; "and then we'll give away the old cash-box. If grand-father had only told us what he was going to do, at first, he need never have used it; for you could have made him a new box beforehand. But, never mind, make it quick now."

Oh, "Julius Cæsar;" strictly obey your little betrothed in this, as in all other injunctions! You know not how soon that new box may be needed, or how much evil it may yet prevent!

CHAPTER V.

CHUMMY DICK.

Perhaps, by this time, you are getting tired of three such simple, homely characters as Mr. and Miss Wray, and Mr. "Julius Cæsar," the carpenter. I strongly suspect you, indeed, of being downright anxious to have a little literary stimulant provided in the shape of a villain. You shall taste this stimulant—double distilled; for I have two villains all ready for you in the present chapter.

But, take my word for it, when you know your new company, you will be only too glad to get back again to Mr. Wray and his family.

About three miles from Tidbury-on-the-Marsh, there is a village called Little London; sometimes popularly entitled, in allusion to the characters frequenting it, "Hell-end." It is a dirty, ruinous-looking collection of some dozen cottages, and an ale-house. Ruffianly men, squalid women, filthy children are its inhabitants. The chief support of this pleasant population is currently supposed to be derived from their connection with the poaching and petty larcenous interests of their native soil. In a word, Little London looks bad, smells bad, and is bad; a fouler blot of a village in the midst of a prettier surrounding landscape, is not to be found in all England.

Our principal business is with the ale-house. The "Jolly Plough-boys" is the sign; and Judith Grimes, widow, the proprietor. The less said about Mrs. Grimes' character, the better; it is not quite adapted to bear discussion in these pages. Mrs. Grimes' mother (who is now bordering on eighty) may be also dismissed to merciful oblivion; for, at her daughter's age, she was—if possible—rather the worse of the two. Towards her son, Mr. Benjamin Grimes, (as one of the rougher sex,) I feel less inclined to be compassionate. When I assert that he was in every respect a complete specimen of a provincial scoundrel, I am guilty, according to a profound and reasonable maxim of our law, of uttering a great libel, because I am repeating a great truth.

You know the sort of man well. You have seen the great, hulking, heavy-browed, sallow-complexioned fellow often enough, lounging at village corners, with a straw in his mouth and a bludgeon in his hand. Perhaps you have asked your way of him, and have been answered by a growl and a petition for money; or, you have heard of him in connection with a cowardly assault on your rural policeman; or a murderous fight with your friend's game-keeper; or a bad case for your other friend, the magistrate, at petty sessions. Anybody who has ever been in the country, knows the man—the ineradical plague-spot of his whole neighborhood—as well as I do.

About eight o'clock in the evening, and on the same day which had been signalized by Mr. Wray's disclosures, Mrs. Grimes, senior—or, as she was generally called, "Mother Grimes"—sat in her armchair in the private parlor of The Jolly Ploughboys, just making up her mind to go to bed. Her ideas on this subject rather wanted acceleration, and they got it from her dutiful son, Mr. Benjamin Grimes.

"Coom, old 'ooman, why doesn't thee trot up stairs?" demanded this provincial worthy.

"I'm a-going, Ben—gently, Judith—I'm a-going!" mumbled the old woman, as Mrs. Grimes, junior, entered the room, and very unceremoniously led her mother off.

"Mind thee doesn't let nobody in here to-night," bawled Benjamin, as his sister went out. "Chummy Dick's going to coom," he added, in a mysterious whisper.

Left to himself to await the arrival of Chummy Dick, Mr. Grimes found time hang rather heavy on his hands. He first looked out of the window. The view commanded a few cottages and fields, with a wood beyond on the rising ground—a homely scene enough in itself; but the heavenly purity of the shining moonlight gave it, just now, a beauty not its own. This beauty was not apparently to the taste of Mr. Grimes, for he quickly looked away from the window back into the room. Staring dreamily, his sunken sinister grey eyes fixed upon the opposite wall, encountering there nothing but four colored prints, representing the career of the prodigal son. He had seen them hundreds of times before; but he looked at them again from mere habit.

In the first of the series, the prodigal son was clothed in a bright red dress coat, and was just getting on horseback (the wrong side;) while his father, in a bright red dress coat, helped him on with one hand, and pointed disconsolately with the other to a cheese-colored road leading straight from the horse's fore-feet to a distant city in the horizon, entirely composed of towers. In the second plate, master prodigal was feasting between two genteel ladies, holding gold wine glasses in their hands; while a debauched companion sprawled on the ground by his side, in a state of cataleptic drunkenness. In the third, he lay on his back; his red coat torn, and showing his purple skin; one of his stockings off; a thunder-storm raging over his head, and two white sows standing on either side of him—one of them apparently feeding off the calf of his leg. In the fourth—

Just as Mr. Grimes had got to the fourth print, he heard somebody whistling a tune outside and turned to the window. It was Chummy Dick; or, in other words, the man with the cat-skin cap, who had honored Mr. Wray with a morning call.

Chummy Dick's conduct on entering the parlor had the merit of originality as an exhibition of manners. He took no more notice of Mr. Grimes than if he had not been in the room; drew his chair to the fire-place; put one foot on each of the hobs; pulled a little card out of his great-coat pocket; read it; and then indulged himself in a long, steady, unctuous fit of laughter, cautiously pitched in what musicians would call the "minor key."

"What dost thee laugh about like that?" asked Grimes.

"Git us a glass of 'ot grog fust—two lumps o'sugar, mind—and then, Benjamin, you'll know in no time!" said Chummy Dick, maintaining an undercurrent of laughter all the while he spoke.

While Benjamin is gone for the grog, there is time enough for a word or two of explanation.

Possibly you may remember that the young assistant at Messrs. Dunball and Dark's happened to see Mr. Wray carrying his cash-box into No. 12. The same gust of wind which, by blowing aside old Reuben's cloak, betrayed what he had got under it to this assistant, exposed the same thing, at the same time, to the observation of Mr. Grimes, who happened to be lounging about the High Street on the occasion in question. Knowing nothing about either the mask or the mystery connected with it, it was only natural that Benjamin should consider the cash-box to be a receptacle for cash; and it was, furthermore, not at all out of character that he should ardently long to be possessed of that same cash, and should communicate his desire to Chummy Dick.

And for this reason. With all the ambition to be a rascal of first-rate ability, Mr. Grimes did not possess the necessary cunning and capacity, and had not received the early London education requisite to fit him for so exalted a position. Stealing poultry out of a farm-yard, for instance, was quite in Benjamin's line; but stealing a cash-box out of a barred and bolted up house, standing in the middle of a large town, was an achievement above his power—an achievement that but one man in his circle of acquaintance was mighty enough to compass—and that man was Chummy Dick, the great London house-breaker. Certain recent passages in the life of this illustrious personage had rendered London and its neighborhood very insecure, in his case, for purposes of residence; so he had retired to a safe distance in the provinces, and had selected Tidbury and the adjacent country as a suitable field for action, and a very pretty refuge from the Bow street runners into the bargain.

"Wery good, Benjamin, and not too sveet," remarked Chummy Dick, tasting the grog which Grimes had brought him. He was not, by any means, one of your ferocious house-breakers, except under strong provocation. There was more of oil than of aquafortis in the mixture of his temperament. His robberies were marvels of skill, cunning and cool determination. In short, he stole plate or money out of dwellinghonses, as cats steal cream off breakfast-tables—by biding his time, and never making a noise.

"Hast thee seen the cash-box?" asked Grimes, in an eager whisper.

"Look at my 'and, Benjamin," was the serenely triumphant answer. "It's bin on the cash-box! You're all right; the swag's ready for us."

"Swag! Wot be that?"

"That's swag!" said Chummy Dick, pulling half-a-crown out of his pocket, and solemnly holding it up for Benjamin's inspection. "I haven't got a fi' pun' note, or a christenin' mug about me; but notes and silver's swag, too. Now, young Grimes, you knows swag; and you'll have your swag before long, if you looks out sharp. If it ain't quite so fine a night to-morrer—if there ain't quite so much of that moonshine as there is now to let gratis for nothin'—why, we'll 'ave the cash-box!"

"Half on it for me! Thee knows't that Chummy Dick!"

"Check that ere talky-talky tongue of your'n; and you'll 'ave your 'alf. I've bin to see the old man; and he's gived me his wisitin' card, with the number of the 'ouse. Ho! hol ho! think of his givin' his card to me! It's as good as inwitin' one to break into the 'ouse—it is, every bit!" And, with another explosion of laughter, Chummy Dick triumphantly threw Mr. Wray's card into the fire.

"But that ain't the pint," he resumed, when he had recovered his breath. "We'll stick to the pint—the pint's the cash-box." And, to do him justice, he did stick to the point, never straying away from it, by so much as a hair's breadth, for a full half-hour.

The upshot of the long harangue to which he now treated Mr. Benjamin Grimes, was briefly this: he had invented a plan, after reading the old man's advertisement first, for getting into Mr. Wray's lodgings unsuspected; he had seen the cash-box with his own eyes, and was satisfied, from certain indicatlons, that there was

44

money in it—he held the owner of this property to be a miser, whose gains were all hoarded up in his cash-box, stray shillings and stray sovereigns together—he had next found out who were the inmates of the house; and had discovered that the only formidable person sleeping at No. 12 was our friend the carpenter—he had then examined the premises, and had seen that they were easily accessible by the back drawing-room window, which looked out on the wash-house roof—finally, he had ascertained that the two watchmen appointed to guard the town, performed that duty by going to bed regularly at eleven o'clock, and leaving the town to guard itself, the whole affair was perfectly easy—too easy, in fact, for anybody but a young beginner.

"Now, Benjamin," said Chummy Dick, in conclusion—"mind this; no wiolence! Take your swag quiet, and you takes it safe. Wiolence is sometimes as bad as knockin' up a whole street—violence is the downy cracksman's last kick-out when he's caught in a fix. Fust and foremost, you've got your mask," (here he pulled out a shabby domino mask,) wery good; nobody can't swear to you in that. Then, you've got your barker," (he produced a pistol,) "just to keep'em quiet with the look of it, and if that want do, there's your gag and bit o' rope" (he drew them forth,) "for their mouths and 'ands. Never pull your trigger, till you see another man ready to pull his. Then you must make your row; and then you make it to some purpose. The nobs in our business—remember this, young Grimes—always takes the swag easy; and when they can't take it easy, they takes it as easy as they can. That's visdom—the visdom of life!"

"Why thee bean't a going, man?" asked Benjamin in astonishment, as the philosophical housebreaker abruptly moved towards the door.

"Me and you mustn't be seen together, to-morrer," said Chummy Dick, in a whisper. "You let me alone; I've got business to do to-night—never mind wot! At eleven to-morrer night, you be at the cross roads that meets on the top of the common. Look out sharp; and you'll see me."

"But if so be it do keep moon-shiny," suggested Grimes.

"On second thoughts, Benjamin," said the housebreaker, after a moment's reflection, "we'll risk all the moonshine as ever shone— High street, Tidbury, ain't Bow street, London—we may risk it safe. Moon, or no moon, young Grimes! to-morrer night's our night!"

By this time he had walked out of the house. They separated at the door. The radiant moon-light falling lovely on all things, fell lovely even on them. How pure it was! how doubly pure, to shine on Benjamin Grimes and Chummy Dick, and not be soiled by the contact!

CHAPTER VI.

A MORNING VISIT.

During the whole remainder of Annie's birth-day, Mr. Wray sat at home, anxiously expecting the promised communication from the mysterious new pupil whose elocution wanted so much setting to rights. Though he never came, and never wrote, old Reuben still persisted in expecting him forthwith; and still waited for him as patiently the next morning, as he had the day before.

Annie sat in the room with her grand-father, occupied in making lace. She had learnt this art, so as to render herself, if possible, of some little use in contributing to the general support; and, sometimes, her manufacture actually poured a few extra shillings into the scantily filled family coffer. Her lace was not at all the sort of thing that your fine people would care to look at twice—it was just simple and pretty, like herself, and only sold (when it did sell, and that, alas! was not often,) among ladies whose purses were very little better furnished than her own.

"Julius Cæsar" was down stairs, in the back kitchen, making the all-important box—or, as the landlady irritably phrased it, "making a mess about the house." She was not partial to saw-dust and shavings, and almost lost her temper when the glue-pot invaded the kitchen fire. But work away, honest carpenter! work away, and never mind her! Get the mask of Shakspeare out of the old box, and into the new, before night comes; and you will have done the best day's work you ever completed in your life!

Annie and her grand-father had a great deal of talk about the Shakspeare cast, while they were sitting together in the drawing-room. If I were to report all old Reuben's rhapsodies and quotations during that period, I might fill the whole remaining space accorded to me in this little book. It was only once that the conversation varied at all. Annie just asked, by way of changing the subject a little, how a plaster cast was taken from the mould; and Mr. Wray instantly went off at a tangent in the midst of a new quotation, to tell her. He was still describing, for the second time, how the plaster and water were to be mixed, how the mixture was to be left to "set," and how the mould was to be pulled off it, when the landlady, looking very hot and important, bustled into the room, exclaiming:

"Mr. Wray, sir! Mr. Wray! Here's Squire Colebatch, of Cropley Court, coming up stairs to see you!" She then added, in a whisper: "He's very hot-tempered and odd, sir, but the best gentleman in the world—"

"That will do, ma'am! that will do!" interrupted a hearty voice, outside the door. "I can introduce myself; an old play-writer and old play-actor don't want much introduction, I fancy! How are you, Mr. Wray? I've come to make your acquaintance; how do you do, sir!"

Before the Squire came in, Mr. Wray's first idea was that the young gentleman pupil had arrived at last—but when the Squire appeared, he discovered that he was mistaken. Mr. Colebatch was an old gentleman with a very rosy face, with bright black eyes that twinkled incessantly, and with perfectly white hair, growing straight up from his head in a complete forest of venerable bristles. Moreover, his elocution wanted no improvement at all; and his "delivery" proclaimed itself at once, as the delivery of a gentleman—a very eccentric one, but a gentleman still.

"Now, Mr. Wray," said the Squire, sitting down, and throwing open his great-coat, with the air of an old friend; "I've a habit of speaking to the point, because I hate ceremony and botheration. My name's Matthew Colebatch; I live at Cropley Court, just outside the town, and I come to see you, because I've had an argument about your character with the Reverend Daubeny Daker, the rector here!"

Astonishment bereft Mr. Wray of all power of speech, while he listened to this introductory address.

"I'll tell you how it was, sir," continued the Squire. "In the first place, Daubeny Daker's a canting sneak—a sort of fellow who goes into poor people's cottages, asking what they've got for dinner, and when they fell him, he takes the cover off the saucepan and sniffs at it, to make sure that they've spoken the truth. That's what he calls doing his duty to the poor, and what I call being a canting sneak! Well, Daubeny Daker saw your advertisement in Dunball's shop window. I must tell you, by-the-by, that he calls theatres the devil's houses, and actors the devil's missionaries; I heard him say that in a sermon, and have never been into his church since! Well, sir, he read your advertisement; and when he came to that part about improving clergymen at three-and six pence an hour, (it would be damned cheap to improve Daubenny Baker at that price,) he falls into one of his nasty, cold blooded, sneering rages, goes into the shop, and insists on having the thing taken down, as as insult offered by a vagabond actor to the clerical character—don't lose your temper, Mr. Wray, don't, for God's sake—I trounced him about it handsomely, I can promise you! And now, what do you think that fat jackass Dunball did, when he heard what the parson said? Took your card down—took it out of the window directly, as if Daubeny Daker was King of Tidbury, and it was death to disobey him!"

"My character, sir!" interposed Mr. Wray.

"Stop, Mr. Wray! I beg your pardon; but I must tell you how I trounced him. Half an hour after the thing had been taken down, I dropped into the shop. Dunball, smiling like a fool, tells me about the business. 'Put it up again, directly!' said I; 'I won't have any man's character bowled down like that by people who don't know him!' Dunball makes a wry face and hesitates. I pull out my watch, and say to him, 'I give you a minute to decide between my custom and interest, and Daubeny Daker's.' I happen to be what's called a rich man, Mr. Wray; so Dunball decided in about two seconds, and up went your advertisement again, just where it was before!"

"I have no words, sir, to thank you for your kindness," said poor old Reuben.

"Hear how I trounced Daubeny Daker, sir—hear that! I met him out at dinner, the same night. He was talking about you, and what he'd done—as proud as a peacock! 'In fact,' says he, at the end of his speech, 'I considered it my duty, as a clergyman, to have the advertisement taken down.' 'And I considered it my duty, as a gentleman,' said I, 'to have it put up again.' Then, we began the argument, (he hates me, because I once wrote a play—I know he does.) I won't tell you what he said, because it would distress you. But it ended, after we'd been at it, hammer and tongs, for about an hour, by my saying that his conduct in setting you down as a disreputable character, without making a single inquiry about you, showed a want of Christianity, justice, and common sense. 'I can bear with your infirmities of temper, Mr. Colebatch,' says he, in his nasty, sneering way; 'but allow me to ask, do you, who defend Mr. Wray so warmly, know any more of him than I do?' He thought this was a settler; but I was at him again, quick as lightning. 'No, sir; but I'll set you a proper example, by going to-morrow morning and judging of the man from the man himself!" That was a settler for him; and now, here I am this morning, to do what I said."

"I will show you, Mr. Colebatch, that I have deserved the honor of being defended by you," said Mr. Wray, with a mixture of artless dignity and manly gratitude in his manner, which became him wonderfully; "I have a letter, sir, from the late Mr. Kemble—"

"What, my old friend, John Philip!" cried the Squire; "let's see it instantly! He, Mr. Wray, was 'the noblest Roman of them all,' as Shakspeare says."

Here was an inestimable friend indeed! He knew Mr. Kemble and quoted Shakspeare. Old Reuben could actually have embraced the Squire at that moment; but he contented himself with producing the great Kemble letter.

Mr. Colebatch read it, and instantly declared that, as a certificate of character, it beat all other certificates that ever were written completely out of the field; and established Mr. Wray's reputation as above the reach of all calumny. "It's the most tremendous crusher for Daubeny Daker that ever was composed, sir!" Just as the old gentleman said this, his eyes encountered little Annie, who had been sitting quietly in the corner of the room, going on with her lace. He had hardly allowed himself leisure enough to look at her, in the first heat of his introductory address, but he made up for lost time now, with characteristic celerity.

"Who's that pretty little girl?" said he; and his bright eyes twinkled more than ever as he spoke.

"My grand-daughter, Annie," answered Mr. Wray, proudly.

"Nice little thing! how pretty and quiet she sits making her lace!" cried Mr. Colebatch, enthusiastically. "Don't move, Annie; don't go away! I like to look at you! You won't mind a queer old bachelor, like me—will you? You'll let me look at you—wou't you? Go on with your lace, my dear, and Mr. Wray and I will go on with our chat."

This "chat" completed what the Kemble letter had begun. Encouraged by the Squire, old Reuben artlessly told the little story of his life, as if to an intimate friend; and told it with all the matchless pathos of simplicity and truth. What time Mr. Colebatch could spare from looking at Annie—and that was not much—he devoted to anathematizing his implacable enemy, Daubeny Daker, in a series of violent expletives; and anticipating, with immense glee, the sort of consummate "troucing" he should now be able to inflict on that reverend gentleman, the next time he met with him. Mr. Wray only wanted to take one step more after this in the Squire's estimation, to be considered the phoenix of all professors of elocution, past, present and future; and he took it. He actually recollected the production of Mr. Colebatch's play—a tragedy all bombast and bloodshed—at Drury Lane Theatre, and more than than that, he had himself performed one of the minor characters in it.

The Squire seized his hand immediately. This play (in virtue of which he considered himself a dramatic author) was his weak point. It had enjoyed a very interrupted "run" of one night; and had never been heard of after. Mr. Colebatch attributed this circumstance entirely to public misappreciation; and, in his old age, boasted of his tragedy wherever he went, utterly regardless of the reception it had met with. It has often been asserted that the parents of sickly children are the parents who love their children best. This remark is sometimes, and only sometimes, true. Transfer it, however, to the sickly children of literature, and it directly becomes a rule which the experience of the whole world is powerless to confute by a single exception!

"My dear sir!" cried Mr. Colebatch, "your remembrance of my play is a new bond between us! It was entitled—of course you recollect—'The Mysterious Murderess.' Gad, sir, do you happen to call to mind the last four lines of the guilty Lindamira's death-scene? It ran thus, Mr. Wray:

Murder and midnight hail! Come all ye horrors!

My soul's congenial darkness quite defies ye!

I'm sick with guilt—What is to cure me? This! (*Stabs herself.*)

Ha! ha! I'm better now—*smiles* (*faintly*)—I'm comfortable!' (*Dies.*)

"If that's not pretty strong writing, sir, my name's not Matthew Colebatch! and yet the besotted audience failed to appreciate it! Bless my soul!" (pulling out his watch,) "one o'clock, already! I ought to be at home! I must go directly. Good-bye, Mr. Wray. I'm so glad to have seen you, that I could almost thank Daubeny Daker for putting me in the towering passion that sent me here. You remind me of my young days, when I used to go behind the scenes, and sup with Kemble and Matthews. Good-bye, little Annie. I'm a wicked old fellow, and I mean to kiss you some day! Not a step further, Mr. Wray; not a step, by George, sir; or I'll never come again. I mean to make the Tidbury people employ your talents; they're the most infernal set of asses under the canopy of heaven; but they shall employ them! I'll engage you to read my play, if nothing else will do, at the Mechanics' Institution. We'll make their flesh creep, sir; and their hair stand on end, with a little tragedy of the good old school. Good-bye, till I see you again, and God bless you!" And away the talkative old squire went, in a mighty hurry, just as he had come in.

"Oh, grand-father, what a nice old gentleman!" exclaimed Annie, looking up for the first time from her lace cushion.

"What unexampled kindness to me! What perfect taste in everything! Did you hear him quote Shakspeare?" cried old Reuben, in an ecstasy. They went on, alternately, in this way, with raptures about Mr. Colebatch, for something like an hour. After that time, Annie left her work, and walked to the window.

"It's raining—raining fast," she said. "Oh, dear, we can't have our walk to-day!"

"Hark! there's the wind moaning," said the old man. "It's getting colder, too. Annie, we are going to have a stormy night."

* * * * * * *

Four o'clock! And the carpenter still at his work in the back kitchén. Faster, "Julius Cæsar," faster. Let us have that mask of Shakspeare out of Mr. Wray's cash-box, and snugly ensconced in your neat wooden casket, before anybody goes to bed tonight. Faster, man— faster.

CHAPTER VII.

A NIGHT VISIT.

For some household reason not worth mentioning, they dined later that day than usual at No. 12. It was five o'clock before they sat down to table. The conversation all turned on the visitor of the morning; no terms in Mr. Wray's own vocabulary, being anything like choice enough to characterize the eccentric old squire, he helped himself to Shakspeare, even more largely than usual, every time he spoke of Mr. Colebatch. He managed to discover some striking resemblance to that excellent gentleman (now in one particular, and now in another,) in every noble and venerable character, throughout the whole series of the plays—not forgetting either, on one or two occasions, to trace the corresponding likeness between the more disreputable and intriguing personages, and that vindictive enemy to all plays, players, and play-houses, the Reverend Daubeny Daker. Never did any professed commentator on Shakspeare (and the assertion is a bold one) wrest the poet's mighty meaning more dexterously into harmony with his own microscopic ideas, than Mr. Wray now wrested it, to furnish him with eulogies on the goodness and generosity of Mr. Matthew Colebatch, of Cropley Court.

Meanwhile, the weather got worse and worse, as the evening advanced. The wind freshened almost to a gale; and dashed the fast falling rain against the window, from time to time, with startling violence. It promised to be one of the wildest, wettest, darkest nights they had had at Tidbury since the winter began.

Shortly after the table was cleared, having pretty well exhausted himself on the subject of Mr. Colebatch, for the present, old Reuben fell asleep in his chair. This was rather an unusual indulgence for him, and was probably produced by the especial lateness of the dinner. Mr. Wray generally took that meal at two o'clock, and set off for his walk afterwards, reckless of all the ceremonial observances of digestion. He was a poor man, and could not afford the luxurious distinction of being dyspeptic.

The Stolen Mask; or, The Mysterious Cash-Box

The behavior of Mr. "Julius Cæsar," the carpenter, when he appeared from the back kitchen to take his place at dinner, was rather perplexing. He knocked down a salt-cellar; spirted some gravy over his shirt; and spilt a potato, in trying to transport it a distance of about four inches, from the dish to Annie's plate. This, to begin with, was rather above the general average of his number of table accidents at one meal. Then, when dinner was over, he announced his intention of returning to the back kitchen for the rest of the evening, in tones of such unwonted mystery, that Annie's curiosity was aroused, and she began to question him. Had he not done the new box yet? No! Why, he might have made such a box in an hour, surely? Yes, he might. And why had he not? "Wait a bit, Annie, and you'll see." And having said that, he laid his large finger mysteriously against the side of his large nose, and walked out of the room forthwith. In half an hour afterwards he came in again looking very sheepish and discomposed, and trying unsuccessfully to hide an enormous poultice—a perfect loaf of warm bread and water—which decorated the palm of his right hand. This time, Annie insisted on an explanation.

It appeared that he had conceived the idea of ornamenting the lid of the new box with some uncouth carvings of his own, in compliment to Mr. Wray and the mask of Shakspeare. Being utterly unpractised in the difficult handiwork he proposed to perform, he had run a splinter into the palm of his hand. And there the box was now in the back kitchen, waiting for lock and hinges, while the only person in the house who could put them on, was not likely to handle a hammer again for days to come. Miserable "Julius Cæsar!" Never was well-meant attention more fatally misdirected than this attention of yours! Of all the multifarious accidents of your essentially accidental life, this special casualty, which has hindered you from finishing the new box to-night, is the most ill-timed and the most irreparable.

When the tea came in, Mr. Wray woke up; and as it usually happens with people who seldom indulge in the innocent sensuality of an after dinner nap, changed at once, from a state of extreme somnolence to a state of extreme wakefulness. By this time the night was at its blackest; the rain fell fierce and thick, and the wild wind walked abroad in the darkness, in all its might and glory. The storm began to affect Annie's spirits a little, and she hinted as much to her grand-father, when he awoke. Old Reuben's extraordinary vivacity immediately suggested a remedy for this. He proposed to read a play of Shakspeare's, as the surest mode of diverting attention from the weather; and, without allowing a moment for the consideration of his offer, he threw open the book, and began "Macbeth."

As he not only treated his hearers to every one of the Kemble pauses, and every infinitesimal inflection of the Kemble elocution, throughout the reading, but also exhibited a serious parody of Mrs. Siddons' effects in Lady Macbeth's sleep-walking scene, with the aid of a white pocket handkerchief, tied under his chin, and a japanned bed-room candle-stick in his hand—and as, in addition to these special and strictly dramatic delays, he further hindered the progress of his occupation by vigilantly keeping his eye on "Julius Cæsar," and unmercifully waking up that ill-starred carpenter every time he went to sleep, (which, by the way, was once in every ten minues,) nobody can be surprised to hear that Macbeth was not finished before eleven o'clock. The hour was striking from Tidbury Church, as Mr. Wray solemnly declaimed the last lines of the tragedy, and shut up the book.

"There!" said old Reuben, "I think I've put the weather out of your head, Annie, by this time. You look sleepy, my dear; go to bed. I had a few remarks to make, about the right reading of Macbeth's dagger-scene, but I can make them to morrow morning, just as well. I won't keep you up any longer. Good night, love!"

Was Mr. Wray not going to bed, too? No; he never felt more awake in his life; he would sit up a little, and have a good "warm" over the fire. Should Annie bear him company? By no means, he would not keep poor Annie from her bed, on any account. Should "Julius Coesar?" Certainly not, he was sure to go to sleep immediately; and to hear him snore, Mr. Wray said, was worse than hearing him sneeze. So the two young people wished the old man good-night, and left him to have his "warm," as he desired. This was the way in which he prepared himself to undergo that luxurious process:

He drew his arm-chair in front of the fire, then put a chair on either side of it, then unlocked the cupboard, and took out the cash-box that contained the mask of Shakspeare. This he deposited upon one of the side chairs; and upon the other he put his copy of the plays, and the candle. Finally, he sat down in the middle—cosy beyond all description—and slowly inhaled a copious pinch of snuff.

"How it blows, outside!" said old Reuben, "and how snug I am, in here!"

He unlocked the cash-box, and taking it on his knee, looked down on the mask that lay inside. Gradually, the pride and pleasure at first appearing in his eyes, gave place to a dreamy fixed expression. He gently closed the lid, and reclined back in his chair; but he did not shut up the cash-box for the night, for he never turned the key in the lock.

Old recollections were crowding on him, revived by his conversation of the morning with Mr. Colebatch; and now evoked by many a Shakspeare association of his own, always connected with the treasured, the inestimable mask. Tender remembrances spoke piteously and solemnly within him. Poor Columbine—lost, but never forgotten—moved loveliest and holiest of all those memory-shadows, through the dim world of his waking visions. How little the grave can hide of us! The love that began before it, lasts after it. The sunlight to which our eyes looked, while it shone on earth, changes but to the star that guides our memories when it passes to heaven!

Hark, the church-clock chimes the quarters; each stroke sounds with the ghostly wildness of all bell-tones, when heard amid the tumult of a storm, but fails to startle old Reuben now. He is far away in other scenes; living again in other times. Twelve strikes; and then, when the clock-bell rings its long midnight peal, he rouses—he hears that.

The fire has died down to one dull, red spot; he feels chilled; and sitting up in his chair, yawning, tries to summon resolution enough to rise and go up stairs to bed. His expression is just beginning to grow utterly listless and weary, when it suddenly alters. His eyes look eager again; his lips close firmly; his cheeks get pale all at once—he is listening. He fancies that, when the wind blows in the loudest gusts, or when the rain dashes heaviest against the window, he hears a very faint, curious sound—sometimes like a scraping noise, sometimes like a tapping noise. But in what part of the house—or even whether outside or in—he cannot tell. In the calmer moments of the storm, he listens with especial attention to find this out; but it is always at that very time that he hears nothing.

It must be imagination. And yet, that imagination is so like a reality that it has made him shudder all over twice in the last minute.

Surely he hears that strange noise now! Why not get up, and go the window, and listen if the faint tapping comes by any chance from outside, in front of the house? Something seems to keep him in his chair, perfectly motionless—something makes him afraid to turn his head, for fear of seeing a sight of horror close at his side——

Hush, it sounds again, plainer and plainer. And now it changes to a cracking noise—close by—at the shutter of the back drawing-room window.

What is that, sliding along the crack between the folding doors and the floor?—a light!—a light in that empty room which nobody uses. And now, a whisper—footsteps—the handle on the lock of the door moves——

"Help, help, for God's sake! Murder! Mur——"

Just as that cry for help passed the old man's lips, the two robbers, masked and armed, appeared in the room; and the next instant Chummy Dick's gag was fast over his mouth.

He had the cash-box clasped tight to his breast. Mad with terror, his eyes glared like a dead man's, while he struggled in the powerful arms that held him.

Grimes, unused to such scenes, was so petrified by astonishment at finding the old man out of bed, and the room lit up, that he stood with his pistol extended, staring helplessly through the eye-holes of his mask. Not so with his experienced leader. Chummy Dick's ears and eyes were as quick as his hands—the first informed him that Reuben's cry for help (skilfully as he had stifled it with the gag) had aroused some one in the house; the second instantly detected the cash-box, as Mr. Wray clasped it to his breast.

"Put up your pop-gun, you precious yokel, you!" whispered the housebreaker fiercely. "Look alive; and pull it out of his arms. Damn you, do it quick! they're awake, up stairs!"

It was not easy to "do it quick." Weak as he was, Reuben actually held his treasure with the convulsive strength of despair, against the athletic ruffian who was struggling to get it away. Furious at the resistance, Grimes exerted his whole force, and tore the box so savagely from the old man's grasp, that the mask of Shakspeare flew several feet away, through the open lid, before it fell, shattered into fragments on the floor.

For an instant, Grimes stood aghast at the sight of what the contents of the cash-box really were. Then, frantic with the savage passions produced by the discovery, he rushed up to the fragments, and, with a horrible oath, stamped his heavy boot upon them, as if the very plaster could feel his vengeance. "I'll kill him, if I swing for it!" cried the villain, turning on Mr. Wray the next moment, and raising his horse-pistol by the barrel over the old man's head.

But, exactly at the same time, brave as his heroic namesake, "Julius Cæsar" burst into the room. In the heat of the moment, he struck at Grimes with his wounded hand. Dealt even under that disadvantage, the blow was heavy enough to hurl the fellow right across the room, till he dropped down against the opposite wall. But the triumph of the stout carpenter was a short one. Hardly a second after his adversary had fallen, he himself lay stunned on the floor by the pistol-butt of Chummy Dick.

Even the nerve of the London housebreaker deserted him, at the first discovery of the astounding self-deception of which he and his companion had been the victims. He only recovered his characteristic coolness and self-possession when the carpenter attacked Grimes. Then, true to his system of never making unnecessary noise, or wasting unnecessary powder, he hit "Julius Cæsar" just behind the ear, with unerring dexterity. The blow made no sound, and seemed to be inflicted by a mere turn of the wrist; but it was decisive—he had thoroughly stunned his man.

And now, the piercing shrieks of the landlady, from the bed-room floor, poured quicker and quicker into the street, through the opened window. They were mingled with the fainter cries of Annie, whom the good woman forcibly detained from going into danger down stairs. The female servant (the only other inmate of the house) rivalled her mistress in shrieking madly and incessantly for help, from the window of the garret above.

"The whole street will be up in a crack!" cried Chummy Dick, swearing at every third word he uttered, and hauling the partially-recovered Grimes into an erect position again; "there's no swag to be got here, step out quick, young yokel, or you'll be nabbed!

He pushed Grimes into the back drawing-room; hustled him over the window-sill on to the wash-house roof, leaving him to find his own way, how he could, to the ground; and then followed, with Mr. Wray's watch and purse, and a brooch of Annie's that had been left on the chimney-piece, all gathered into his capacious great-coat pocket in a moment. They were not worth much as spoils; but the dexterity with which they were taken instantly with one hand, while he had Grimes to hold with the other; and the strength, coolness, and skill he displayed in managing the retreat, were worthy even of the reputation of Chummy Dick. Long before the two Tidbury watchmen had begun to think of a pursuit, the housebreaker and his companion were out of reach—even though the Bow street runners themselves had been on the spot to give chase.

* * * * * *

How long the old man has kept in that one position—crouching down there in the corner of the room, without stirring a limb, or uttering a word. He dropped on his knees at that place, when the robbers left him; and nothing has moved him from it since.

When Annie broke away from the landlady, and ran down stairs— he never stirred. When the long wail of agony burst from her lips, as she saw the dead-look of the brave man lying stunned on the floor— he never spoke. When the street-door was opened; and the crowd of terrified, half-dressed neighbors all rushed together into the house, shouting and trampling about, half panic-stricken at the news they heard—he never noticed a single soul. When the doctor was sent for; and, amid an awful hush of expectation, proceeded to restore the carpenter to his senses—even at that enthralling moment, he never looked up. It was only when the room was cleared again—when his grand-daughter came to his side, and, putting her arm round his neck, laid her cold cheek close to his—that he seemed to live at all. Then, he just heaved a heavy sigh; his head dropped down lower on his breast; and he shivered throughout his whole frame, as if some icy influence was freezing him to the heart.

All that long, long time, he had been looking on one sight—the fragments of the mask of Shakspeare lying beneath him. And there he kept now—when they tried in their various methods to coax him away—still crouching over them; just in the same position; just with the same hard, frightful look about his face that they had seen from the first.

Annie went and fetched the cash-box, and tremblingly put it down before him. The instant he saw it, his eyes began to flash. He pounced in a fury of haste upon the fragments of the mask, and huddled them all together into the box, with shaking hands, and quick panting breath. He picked up the least chip of plaster that the robber had ground under his boot; and strained his eyes to look for more, when not an atom more was left. At last, he locked the box, and caught it up tight to his breast; and then he let them raise him up, and lead him gently away from the place.

He never quitted hold of his box, while they got him into bed. Annie, and her lover, and the land-lady, all sat up together in his room; and all, in different degrees, felt the same horrible foreboding about him, and shrank from communicating it to one another. Occasionally, they heard him beating his hands strangely on the lid of the box; but he never spoke; and, as far as they could discover, never slept.

The doctor had said he would be better when the daylight came. Did the doctor really know what was the matter with him—and had the doctor any suspicion that something precious had been badly injured that night, besides the mask of Shakspeare?

CHAPTER VIII.

A THOUGHT OF ANNIE'S.

By the next morning the news of the burglary had not only spread all through Tidbury, but all through the adjacent villages as well. The very first person who called at No. 12, to see how they did after the fright of the night before, was Mr. Colebatch. The old gentleman's voice was heard louder than ever, as he ascended the stairs with the landlady. He declared he would have both the Tidbury watchmen turned off, as totally unfit to take care of the town. He swore that, if it cost him a hundred pounds, he would fetch the Bow street runners down from London, and procure the catching, trying, convicting, and hanging of "those two infernal house-breakers" before Christmas came. Invoking vengeance and retribution in this way, at every fresh stair, the Squire's temperament was up at "blood-heat," by the time he got into the drawing-room. It fell, directly, however, to "temperate" again, when he found nobody there; and it sank twenty degrees lower still, at the sight of little Annie's face, when she came down to see him.

"Cheer up, Annie!" said the old gentleman, with a last faint attempt at joviality, "It's all over now, you know; how's grand-father? Very much frightened still—eh?"

"Oh, sir! frightened, I'm afraid out of his mind!" and unable to control herself any longer, poor Annie fairly burst into tears.

"Don't cry, Annie, no crying! I can't stand it—you mustn't really!" said the Squire, in anything but steady tones, "I'll talk him back into his mind; I will, as sure as my name's Matthew Colebatch; stop," (here he pulled out his voluminous India pocket-handkerchief, and began very gently and caressingly to wipe away her tears, as if she had been a little child, and his own daughter.) "There, now we've dried them up—no we havn't! there's one left. And now that's gone, let's have a little talk about this business, my dear, and see what's to be done. In the first place, what's all this I hear about a plaster cast being broken?"

Annie would have given the world to open her heart about the mask of Shakspeare, to Mr. Colebatch; but she thought of her promise, and she thought, also, of the town council of Stratford, who might hear of the secret somehow, if it was once disclosed to anybody; and might pursue her grand-father with all the powers of the law, miserable and shattered though he now was, even to his hiding place, at Tidbury-on-the-Marsh.

"I've promised, sir, not to say anything about the plaster-cast to anybody," she began, looking very embarrassed and unhappy.

"And you'll keep your promise," interposed the Squire; "that's right—good, honest little girl! I like you all the better for it; we won't say a word more about the cast; but what have they taken? what have the infernal scoundrels taken?"

"Grand-father's old silver watch, sir, and his purse with seventeen and six-pence in it, and my brooch—but that's nothing."

"Nothing! Annie's brooch nothing!" cried the Squire, recovering his constitutional testiness. "But never mind, I'm determined to have the rascals caught and hung, if it's only for stealing that brooch! And now, look here, my dear; if you don't want to put me into one of my passions, take that and say nothing about it!"

"Take" what? gracious powers! "take" Golconda! he had crumpled a ten pound note into her hand!

"I say, again, you obstinate little thing, don't put me in one of my passions!" exclaimedt he old gentleman, as poor Annie made some faint show of difficulty in taking the gift. "God forbid I should think of hurting your feelings, my dear, for such a paltry reason as having a few more pounds in my pocket, than you have in yours!" he continued, in such serious, kind tones, that Annie's eyes began to fill again. "We'll call that bank note, if you like, payment before hand, for a large order for lace, from me. I saw you making lace, you know, yesterday; and I mean to consider you my lace-manufacturer in ordinary, for the rest of your life. By George"—he went on, resuming his odd abrupt manner—"it's unknown the quantity of lace I shall want to buy! There's my old house-keeper, Mrs. Buddle—hang me, Annie, if I don't dress her in nothing but lace, from top to toe, inside and out, all over! Only mind this, you don't set to work at the order till I tell you! We must wait till Mrs. Buddle has worn out her old stock of petticoats, before we begin—eh? There, there, there, don't go crying again! Can I see Mr. Wray? No? Quite right, better not disturb him so soon. Give him my compliments, and say I'll call to-morrow. Put up the note, put up the note, and don't be low spirited—and don't do another thing, little Annie; don't forget you've got a queer old friend, who lives at Cropley Court!"

Running on in this way, the good Squire fairly talked himself out of the room, without letting Annie get in a word edgewise. Once on the stairs, he fell foul of the house-breakers again, with undiminished fury. The last thing the landlady heard him say, as she closed the street door after him, was, that he was off now, to "trounce" the two Tidbury watchmen, for not stopping the robbery—to "trounce them handsomely," as sure as his name was Matthew Colebatchl

Carefully putting away the kind old gentleman's gift, (they were penniless before she received it,) Annie returned to her grand-father's room. He had altered a little, as the morning advanced, and was now occupied over an employment which it wrung her heart to see—he was trying to restore the mask of Shakspeare.

The first words he had spoken since the burglary, were addressed to Annie. He seemed not to know that the robbers had effected their retreat, before she got down stairs; and asked whether they had hurt her. Calmed on this point, he next beckoned the carpenter to him, and entreated, in an eager whisper, to have some glue made directly. They could not imagine, at first, what he wanted it for; but they humored him gladly.

When the glue was brought, he opened his cash-box, with a look of faint pining hope in his face, that it was very mournful to see, and began to arrange the fragments of the mask on the bed before him. They were shattered past all mending; but still he moved them about here and there, with his trembling hands, murmuring sadly, all the while, that he knew it was very difficult, but felt sure he should succeeed at last. Sometimes he selected the pieces wrongly, stuck, perhaps, two or three together with the glue; and then had to pull them apart again. Even when he chose the fragments properly, he could not find enough that would join sufficiently well to re-produce only one poor quarter of the mask in its former shape. Still he went on, turning over piece after piece of the broken plaster, down to the very smallest, patiently and laboriously, with the same false hope of success, and the same vain perseverance under the most disheartening failure, animating him for hours together. He had begun early in the morning—he had not given up, when Annie returned from her interview with Mr. Colebatch. To know how utterly fruitless all his efforts must be, and still to see him anxiously continuing them in spite of failure, was a sight to despair over, and to tremble at, indeed.

At last, Annie entreated him to put the fragments away in the box, and take a little rest. He would listen to nobody else; but he listened to her, and did what she asked; saying that his head was not clear enough for the work of repairing, to-day; but that he felt certain he should succeed to-morrow. When he had locked the box, and put it under his pillow, he laid back, and fell into a sleep directly.

Such was his condition! Every idea was now out of his mind, but the idea of restoring the mask of Shakspeare. Divert him from that, and he either fell asleep, or sat up vacant and speechless. It was suspension, not loss of the faculties, with him. The fibre of his mind relaxed with the breaking of the beloved possession to which it had been attached. Those still, cold, plaster features had been his thought by day, his dream by night; in them, his deep and beautiful devotion to Shakspeare—beautiful as an innate poetic faith that had lived through every poetic privation of life—had found its dearest outward manifestation. All about that mask, he had unconsciously hung fresh votive offerings of pride and pleasure, and humble happiness, almost with every fresh hour. It had been the one great achievement of his life, to get it; and the one great determination of his life, to keep it. And now it was broken! The dearest household god, next to his grand-child, that the poor actor had ever had to worship, his own eyes had seen lying shattered on the floor!

It was this—far more than the fright produced by the burglary—that had altered him, as he was altered now.

There was no rousing him. Everybody tried, and everybody failed. He went on patiently, day after day, at his miserably hopeless task of joining the fragments of the plaster; and always had some excuse for failure, always some reason for beginning the attempt anew. Annie could influence him in everything else—for his heart, which was all hers, had escaped the blow that had stunned his mind—but, on any subject connected with the mask, her interference was powerless.

The good squire came to try what he could do—came every day; and joked, entreated, lectured and advised, in his own hearty, eccentric manner; but the old man only smiled faintly, and forgot what had been said said to him, as soon as words were out of the sayer's mouth. Mr. Colebatch, reduced to his last resources, hit on what he considered a first-rate stratagem. He privately informed Annie, that he would insist on his whole establishment of servants, with Mrs. Buddle, the housekeeper, at their head, learning elocution; so as to employ Mr. Wray again, in a duty he was used to perform. "None of those infernal Tidbury people will learn," said the kind old squire; "so my servants shall make a class for him, with Mrs. Buddle at the top, to keep them in order. Set him teaching in his own way; and he must come round—he must, from force of habit!" But he did not. They told him a class of new pupils was waiting for him; he just answered he was very glad to hear it; and forgot all about the matter the moment afterwards.

The doctor endeavored to help them. He tried stimulants, and tried sedatives; he tried keeping his patient in bed, and tried keeping him up; he tried blistering, and tried cupping; and then he gave over;

saying that Mr. Wray must certainly have something on his mind, and that physic and regimen were of no use. One word of comfort, however, the doctor still had to speak. The physical strength of the old man had failed him very little, as yet. He was always ready to be got out of bed, and dressed; and seemd glad when he was seated in his chair. This was a good sign; but there was no telling how long it might last.

It lasted a whole week—a long, blank, melancholy winter's week! And now, Christmas Day was fast coming; coming for the first time as a day of mourning, to the little family who, in spite of poverty and all poverty's hardening disasters, had hitherto enjoyed it happily and lovingly together, as the blessed holiday of the whole year! Ah, how doubly heavy-hearted poor Annie felt, as she entered her bed-room for the night, and remembered that day fortnight would be Christmas Day!

She was beginning to look wan and thin already. It is not joy only, that shows soonest and plainest in the young; grief—alas! that it should be so—shares, in this world, the same privilege; and Annie now looked, as she felt, sick at heart. That day had brought no change; she had left the old man for the night, and left him no better. He had passed hours again, in trying to restore the mask; still instinctively exhibiting from time to time some fondness and attention towards his grand child—but just as hopelessly vacant to every other influence as ever.

Annie listlessly sat down on the one chair in her small bed-room, thinking (it was her only thought now) of what new plan could be adopted to rouse her grand-father on the morrow; and still mourning over the broken mask, as the one fatal obstacle to every effort she could try. Thus she sat for some minutes, languid and dreamy—when, suddenly, a startling and a wonderful change came over her, worked from within. She bounded up from her chair, as dead-pale and as dead-still as if she had been struck to stone. Then, a moment after, her face flushed crimson, she clasped her hands violently together, and drew her breath quick. And then, the paleness came once more—she trembled all over—and knelt down by the bed-side, hiding her face in her hands.

When she rose again, the tears were rolling fast over her cheeks. She poured out some water, and washed them away. A strange expression of firmness—a glow of enthusiasm, beautiful in its brightness and purity—overspread her face, as she took up her candle, and left the room.

She went to the very top of the house, where the carpenter slept, and knocked at his door.

"Are you not gone to bed yet, Martin?" she whispered—(the old joke of calling him "Julius Cæsar" was all over now!)

He opened the door in astonishment, saying he had only that moment got up stairs.

"Come down to the drawing-room, Martin," she said, looking brightly on him—almost wildly, as he thought. "Come quick, I must speak to you at once."

He followed her down stairs. When they get into the drawing-room, she carefully closed the door; and then said:

"A thought has come to me, Martin, that I must tell you. It came to me just now, when I was alone in my room; and I believe God sent it!"

She beckoned to him to sit by her side; and then began to whisper in his ear—quickly, eagerly, without pause.

His face began to turn pale at first, as hers had done, while he listened. Then it flushed, then grew firm like hers, but in a far stronger degree. When she had finished speaking, he only said, it was a terrible risk every way—repeating "every way," with strong emphasis; but that she wished it; and therefore it should be done.

As they rose to separate, she said tenderly and gravely:

"You have always been very good to me, Martin; be good, and be a brother to me more than ever now—for now I am trusting you with all I have to trust."

Years afterwards, when they were married, and when their children were growing up around them, he remembered Annie's last look, and Annie's last words, as they parted that night.

CHAPTER IX.

THE MASK OF SHAKSPEARE.

The next morning, when the old man was ready to get out of bed and be dressed, if was not the honest carpenter who came to help him as usual, but a stranger—the landlady's brother. He never noticed this change. What thoughts he had left, were all pre-occupied. The evening before, from an affectionate wish to humor him in the caprice which had become the one leading idea of his life, Annie had bought for him a bottle of cement. And now, he went on murmuring to himself, all the while he was being dressed, about the certainty of his succeeding at last in piecing together the broken fragments of the mask, with the aid of this cement. It was only the glue, he said, that had made him fail hitherto; with cement to aid him, he was quite certain of success.

The landlady and her brother helped him down into the drawing-room. Nobody was there; but on the table, where the breakfast things were laid, was placed a small note. He looked round inquisitively when he first saw that the apartment was empty. Then, the only voice within him that was not silenced—the voice of his heart—spoke, and told him that Annie ought to have been in the room to meet him as usual.

"Where is she?" he asked eagerly.

"Don't leave me alone with him, James," whispered the landlady to her brother, "there's bad news to tell him."

"Where is she?" he reiterated; and his eye got a wild look, as he asked the question for the second time.

"Pray compose yourself, sir; and read that letter," said the landlady, in soothing tones; "Miss Annie's quite safe, and wants you to read this." She handed him the letter.

He struck it away; so fiercely that she started back in terror. Then he cried out violently for the third time,

"Where is she?"

"Tell him," whispered the landlady's brother, tell him at once, or you'll make him worse."

"Gone, sir," said the woman—"gone away; but only for three days. The last words she said were, tell my grand-father I shall be back in three days; and give him that letter with my dearest love. Oh, don't look so, sir—don't look so! She's sure to be back."

He was muttering "gone" several times to himself, with a fearful expression of vacancy in his eyes. Suddenly, he signed to have the letter picked up from the ground; tore it open the moment it was given to him, and began to try to read the contents.

The letter was short, and written in very blotted, unsteady characters. It ran thus:

"DEAREST GRAND-FATHER: I never left you before in my life; and I only go now to try and serve you, and do you good. In three days, or sooner, if God pleases, I will come back, bringing something with me that will gladden your heart, and make you love me even better than ever. I dare not tell you where I am going, or what I am going for—you would be so frightened, and would perhaps send after me to fetch me back; but believe there is no danger! And, oh, dear grand-father, don't doubt your little Annie; and don't doubt I will be back as I say, bringing something to make you forgive me for going away without your leave. We shall be so happy again, if you will only wait the three days! He—you know who—goes with me, to take care of me. Think, dear grand-father, of the blessed Christmas time that will bring us all together again, happier than ever! I can't write any more, but that I pray God to bless and keep you, till we meet again.

ANNIE WRAY."

He had not read the letter more than half through when he dropped it, uttering the one word, "gone," in a shrill scream, that it made them shudder to hear. Then, it seemed as if a shadow, an awful, indescribable shadow, were stealing over his face. His fingers worked and fidgetted with an end of the table-cloth close by him; and he began to speak in faint whispering tones.

"I'm afraid I'm going mad; I'm afraid something's frightened me out of my wits," he murmured, under his breath. "Stop, let me try if I know any thing. There now, there! That's the breakfast-table; I know that. There's her cup and saucer; and there's mine. Yes, and that third place, on the other side, whose is that—whose, whose, whose? Ah, my God, my God, I am mad! I've forgotten that third place!" He stopped, shivering all over. Then, the moment after, he shrieked out—"gone, who says she's gone? It's a lie; no, no, it's a cruel joke put upon me. Annie, I won't be joked with. Come down, Annie! Call her, some of you! Annie, they've broken it all to pieces—the plaster won't stick together again! You can't leave me, now they've broken it all to pieces! Annie, Annie, come and mend it! Annie! little Annie!"

He called on her name for the last time, in tones of entreaty unutterably plaintive; then sank down on a chair, moaning; then became silent— doggedly silent—and fiercely suspicious of everything. In that mood he remained, till his strength began to fail him; and then he let them lead him to the sofa. When he lay down, he fell off quickly into a heavy, feverish slumber.

Ah, Annie, Annie, carefully as you watched him, you knew but little of his illness; you never foreboded such a result of your absence as this; or, brave and loving as your purpose was in leaving him, you would have shrunk from the tatal necessity of quitting his bed-side for three days together!

Mr. Colebatch came in shortly after the old man had fallen asleep, accompanied by a new doctor—a medical man of great renown, who had stolen a little time from his London practice, partly to visit some relations who lived at Tidbury, and partly to recruit his own health, which had suffered in repairing other people's. The good squire, the moment he heard that such assistance as this was accidentally available in the town, secured it for poor old Reuben, without a moment's delay.

"Oh, sir!" said the landlady, meeting them down stairs; "he's been going on in such a dreadful way! What we are to do, I really don't know."

"It's lucky somebody else does," interrupted the squire, peevishly.

"But you don't know, sir, that Miss Annie's gone—gone without saying where!"

"Yes, I happen to know that, too!" said Mr. Colebatch; "I've got a letter from her, asking me to take care of her grand-father, while she's away; and here I am to do what she tells me. First of all, ma'am, let us get into some room, where this gentleman and I can have five minutes talk in private."

"Now, sir"—said the squire, when he and the doctor were closeted together in the back parlor—"the long and the short of the case is this—a week ago, two infernal housebreakers broke into this house, and found old Mr. Wray sitting up alone in the drawing-room. Of course, they frightened him out of his wits; and they stole some trifles, too—but that's nothing. They managed somehow to break a plaster cast of his. There's a mystery about this cast, that the family won't explain, and that nobody can find out; but the fact appears to be, that the old man was as fond of his cast as if it was one of his children—a queer thing, you'll say; but true, sir; true as my name's Colebatch! Well, ever since, he's been weak in his mind; always striving to mend this wretched cast, and taking no notice of any thing else. This sort of thing has lasted for six or seven days. And now, another mystery! I get a letter from his grand-daughter—the kindest, dearest little thing—begging me to look after him—you never saw such a lovely, tender-hearted letter—to look after him, I say, while she's gone for three days, to come back with a surprise for him that she says will work miracles. She don't say what surprise— or where she's going—but she promises to come back in three days;

and she'll do it! I'll stake my existence on little Annie sticking to her word! Now, the question is—till we see her again, and all this precious mystery's cleared up—what are we to do for the poor old man—what—eh?"

"Perhaps"—said the doctor, smiling at the conclusion of this characteristic harangue—"perhaps I had better see the patient, before we say any more."

"By George! what a fool I am!"—cried the squire; "of course—see him directly—this way, doctor; this way!"

They went into the drawing room. The sufferer was still on the sofa, moving and talking in his sleep. The doctor signed to Mr. Colebatch to keep silence; and they sat down and listened.

The old man's dreams seemed to be connected with some of the later scenes in his life, which had been passed in country towns, in teaching country actors. He was laughing just at this moment.

"Ho! ho! young gentlemen"—they heard him say; "do you call that acting? Ah, dear, dear, we professional people don't bump against each other on the stage, in that way—it's lucky you called me in, before your friends came to see you! Stop, sir, that won't do; you mustn't die in that way—fall on your knee first; then sink down—then—oh, dear, how hard it is to get people to have a proper delivery, and not go dropping their voices, at the end of every sentence. I shall never—never—"

Here the wild words stopped; then altered, and grew sad.

"Hush, hush!"—he murmured, in husky, wondering tones—"silence there, behind the scenes! Don't you hear Mr. Kemble speaking now; listen and get a lesson, as I do. Laugh away, fools, who don't know good acting when you see it—let me alone! What are you pushing me for? I'm doing you no harm! I'm only looking at Mr. Kemble—don't touch that book—it's my Shakespeare—yes, mine. I suppose I may read Shakespeare if I like, though I am only an actor at a shilling a night—a shilling a night—starving wages—ha, ha, ha—starving wages!"

Again the sad strain altered to a still wilder and more plaintive key.

"Ah!" he cried now, "don't be hard with me! Don't, for God's sake! My wife, my poor dear wife, died only a week ago! Oh, I'm cold, starved with cold here, in this draughty place. I can't help crying, sir; she was so good to me! But I'll take care and go on the stage when I'm called to go, if you'll please not take any notice of me now, and not let them laugh at me. Oh, Mary, Mary! Why has God taken you from me? Ah, why, why, why!"

Here the murmurs died away; then begain again, but more confusedly. Sometimes his wandering speech was all about Annie; sometimes it changed to lamentations over the broken mask; sometimes it went back again to the old days behind the scenes at Drury Lane.

"Oh, Annie, Annie!" cried the Squire, with his eyes full of tears; "why did you ever go away?"

"I am not sure," said the doctor "that her going may not do good in the end. It has evidently brought matters to a climax with him; I can see that. Her coming back will be a shock to his mind—it's a risk, sir; but that shock may act in the right way. When a man's faculties struggle to recover themselves, as his are doing, those faculties are not altogether gone. The young lady will come back, you say, the day after to-morrow?"

"Yes, yes!" answered the Squire, "with a 'surprise,' she says. What surprise? Good Heavens, why couldn't she say what!"

"We need not mind that," rejoined the other. "Any surprise will do, if his physical strength will bear it. We'll keep him quiet—as much asleep as possible—till she comes back. I've seen some very curious cases of this kind, Mr. Colebatch; cases that were cured by the merest accidents, in the most unaccountable manner. I shall watch this particular case with interest."

"Cure it, doctor, cure it; and, by Jupiter, I'll—"

"Hush, you'll wake him. We had better go now. I shall come back in an hour, and will tell the landlady where she can let me know, if anything happens before that."

They went out softly; and left him as they had found him, muttering and murmuring in his sleep.

* * * * * *

On the third day, late in the afternoon, Mr. Colebatch and the doctor were again in the drawing-room at No. 12, and again intently occupied in studying the condition of poor old Reuben Wray.

This time he was wide awake, and was restlessly and feebly moving up and down the room, talking to himself, now mournfully about the broken mask, now fiercely and angrily about Annie's absence. Nothing attracted his notice in the smallest degree; he seemed to be perfectly unaware that anybody was in the room with him.

"Why can't you keep him quiet?" whispered the Squire; "why don't you give him an opiate, or whatever you call it, as you did yesterday?"

"His grand-child comes back to-day," answered the doctor. "To-day must be left to the great physician—Nature. At this crisis, it is not for me to meddle, but to watch and learn."

They waited again in silence. Lights were brought in; for it grew dark while they kept their anxious watch. Still no arrival!

Five o'clock struck; and, about ten minutes after, a knock sounded at the street door.

"She has come back!" exclaimed the doctor.

"How do you know that already?" asked Mr. Colebatch eagerly.

"Look there, sir!" and the doctor pointed to Mr. Wray.

He had been moving about with increased restlessness, and talking with increased vehemence, just before the knock. The moment it sounded, he stopped; and there he stood now, perfectly speechless and perfectly still. There was no expression on his face. His breathing seemed suspended. What secret influences were moving within him now? What dread command went forth over the dark waters in which his spirit toiled, saying to them, "Peace, be still!" That, no man—not even the man of science—could tell.

As the door opened, and the landlady's joyful exclamation of recognition sounded cheerily from below, the doctor rose from his seat, and gently placed himself close behind the old man.

Footsteps hurried up stairs. Then, Annie's voice was heard, breathless and eager, before she came in. "Grand-father, I've got the mould! Grand-father, I've brought a new cast. The mask—thank God!—the mask of Shakspeare!"

She flew into his arms, without even a look at anybody else in the room. When her head was on his bosom, the spirit of the brave little girl deserted her for the first time since her absence, and she burst into an hysterical passion of weeping before she could utter another word.

He gave a great cry the moment she touched him—an inarticulate voice of recognition from the spirit within. Then his arms closed tight over her; so tight, that the doctor advanced a step or two towards them, showing in his face the first look of alarm it had yet betrayed.

But, at that instant, the old man's arms dropped again, powerless and heavy, by his side. What does he see now, in that open box in the carpenter's hand? The mask!—*his* mask, whole as ever! white and smooth, and beautiful, as when he first drew it from the mould, in his own bed-room at Stratford.

The struggle of the vital principle at that sight—the straining and writhing of every nerve—was awful to look on. His eyes rolled, distended, in their orbits; a dark red flush of blood heaved up and overspread his face; he drew his breath in heavy, hoarse gasps of agony. This lasted for a moment—one dread moment; then he fell forward, to all appearance death-struck, in the doctor's arms.

He was borne to a sofa, amid the silence of that suspense which is too terrible for words. The doctor laid his finger on his wrist, waited an instant, then looked up, and slightly nodded his head. The pulse was feebly beating again, already.

Long and delicate was the process of restoring him to animation. It was like aiding the faint new life to develop itself in a child just born. But the doctor was as patient as he was skillful; and they heard the old man draw his breath again, gently and naturally, at last.

His weakness was so great, that his eye-lids closed at his first effort to look around him. When they opened again, his eyes seemed strangely liquid and soft—almost like the eyes of a young girl. Perhaps this was partly because they turned on Annie the moment they could see.

Soon, his lips moved; but his voice was so faint, that the doctor was obliged to listen close at his mouth to hear him. He said, in fluttering accents, that he had had a *dreadful dream,* which had made him very ill, he was afraid; but that it was all over, and he was better now, though not quite strong enough to receive so many visitors yet. Here his strength for speaking failed, and he looked round on Annie again in silence. In a minute more he whispered to her. She went to the table and fetched the new mask; and, kneeling down, held it before him to look at. The doctor beckoned Mr. Colebatch, the landlady and the carpenter, to follow him into the back room.

"Now," said he, "I've one, and only one, important direction to give you all; and you must communicate it to Miss Wray when she is a little less agitated. On no account let the patient imagine he's wrong in thinking that all his troubles have been the troubles of a dream. That will be the weak point in his intellectual consciousness for the rest of his life. When he gets stronger, he is sure to question you curiously about this dream; keep him in his self-deceit, as you value his sanity! He's only got his reason back by getting it out of the very jaws of death, I can tell you—give it full time to strengthen! You know, I dare say, that a joint which is dislocated by a jerk, is also replaced by a jerk. Consider his mind, in the same way, to have been dislocated by one shock, and now replaced by another; and treat his intellect as you would treat a limb that had only just been slipped back into its proper place—treat it tenderly. By the-bye," added the doctor, after a moment's consideration, "if you can't get the key of his box, without suspicion, pick the lock; and throw away the fragments of the old cast (which he was always talking about in his delirium)—destroy them altogether. If he ever sees them again, they may do him dreadful mischief. He must always imagine what he imagines at present, that the new cast is the same cast that he has had all along. It's a very remarkable case, Mr. Colebatch, very remarkable; I really feel indebted to you for enabling me to study it. Compose yourself, sir; you're a little shaken and startled by this, I see; but there's no danger for him now. Look there: that man, except on one point, is as sane as ever he was in his life!"

They looked, as the doctor spoke. Mr. Wray was still on the sofa, gazing at the mask of Shakspeare, which Annie supported before him, as she knelt by his side. His arm was round her neck; and, from time to time, he whispered to her, smiling faintly, but very happily, as she replied in whispers also. The sight was simple enough; but the landlady, thinking on all that had passed, began to weep as she beheld it. The hones carpenter looked very ready to follow her example; and Mr. Colebatch probably shared the same weakness at that moment, though he was less can did in betraying it. "Come," said the Squire, very huskily and hastily, "we are only in the way here; let us leave them together!"

"Quite right, sir," observed the doctor; "that pretty little girl is the ouly medical attendant fit to be with him now! I wait for you, Mr. Colebatch!"

"I say, young fellow," said the Squire to the carpenter, as they went down stairs, "be in the way to-morrow morning; I've a good deal to ask you in private when I'm not all over in a twitter, as I am at present. Now our good old friend's getting round, my curiosity's getting round too. Be in the way to-morrow, at ten, when I come here. Quite ready, doctor! No, after you, if you please. Ah, thank God, we came into this house mourners, and we go out of it to rejoice. It will be a happy Christmas, doctor, and a merry New Year, after all!"

CHAPTER X.

CHRISTMAS TIME.

When ten o'clock came, the Squire came—punctual to a minute. Instead of going up stairs, he mysteriously sent for the carpenter into the back parlor.

"Now, in the first place, how is Mr. Wray?" said the old gentleman, as anxiously as if he had not already sent three times the night before, and twice earlier in the morning, to ask that very question.

"Lord bless you, sir!" answered the carpenter, with a grin, and a very expressive rubbing of the hands—"he's coming to again, after his nice sleep last night, as brave as ever. He's dreadful weak still, to be sure; but he's got like himself again, already. He's been down on me twice in the last half hour, sir, about my elocution; he's making Annie read Shakspeare to him; and he's asking whether any new pupils are coming—all just in the old way again. Oh, sir, it is so jolly to see him like that once more—if you'll only come up stairs——"

"Stop, till we've had our talk," said the Squire; "sit down. By-the-bye, has he said anything yet about that infernal cash-box?"

"I picked the lock off the box this morning, sir, as the gentleman told me; and buried every bit of plaster out of it, deep in the kitchen garden. He saw the box afterwards, and gave a tremble, like. 'Take it away,' says he, 'never let me see it again; it reminds me of that dreadful dream.' And then, sir, he told us about what had happened, just as if he really had dreamt it; saying he couldn't get the subject quite out of his head, the whole thing was so much as if it had truly taken place. Afterwards, sir, he thanked me for making the new box for the cast—he remembered my promising to do that, though it was only just before all our trouble!"

"And of course, you humor him in everything, let him think he's right?" said the Squire; "he must never know that he hasn't been dreaming, to his dying day."

And he never did know it—never in this world, had even a suspicion of what he owed to Annie! It was but little matter; they could not have loved each other better, if he had discovered everything.

"Now, master carpenter," pursued the Squire, "you've answered very nicely hitherto. Just answer as nicely the next question I ask. What's the whole history of this mysterious plaster cast? It's no use fidgetting! I've seen the cast; I know it's a portrait of Shakspeare! and I have made up my mind to find out all about it. Do you mean to say you think I'm not a friend fit to be trusted? Eh, you sir?".

"I never could think so, after all your goodness, sir. But, if you please, I really did promise to keep the thing a secret," said the carpenter, looking very much as if he were watching his opportunity to open the door, and run out of the room; "I promised, sir; I did, indeed!"

"Promised a fiddlestick!" exclaimed the Squire, in a passion. "What's the use of keeping a secret that's half let out already? I'll tell you what, you Mr.—, what's your name? There's some joke about calling you Julius Cæsar. What's your real name, if you really have one?"

"Martin Blunt, sir. But don't, pray don't, ask me to tell the secret! I don't say you would blab it, sir; but if it did leak out, like; and get to Stratford-upon-Avon"—here he suddenly became silent, feeling he was beginning to commit himself already.

"Stop! I've got it!" cried Mr. Colebatch. "Hang me, if I haven't got it at last."

"Don't tell *me,* sir. Pray don't tell me, if you have!"

"Stick to your chair, Mr. Martin Blunt. No shirking with *me.* I was a fool not to suspect the thing, the moment I saw it was a portrait of

Shakspeare. I've seen the Stratford bust, Master Blunt. You're afraid of Stratford, are you? Why? I know. Some of you have been taking that cast from the Stratford bust, without leave—it's as like it as two peas. Now, young fellow, I'll tell you what, if you don't make a clean breast to me at once, I'm off to the office of the 'Tidbury *Mercury*,' to put in my version of the whole thing, as a good local anecdote Will you tell me? or will you not? I'm asking this in Mr. Wray's interests, or I'd die before I'd ask you at all."

Confused, threatened, bullied, bawled at, and outmanoeuvred, the unfortunate carpenter fairly gave way. "If it's wrong in me to tell you, sir, it's your fault what I do," said the simple fellow; and he forthwith related, in a very roundabout, stammering manner, the whole of the disclosure he had heard from old Reuben—the Squire occasionally throwing in an explosive interjection of astonishment, or admiration; but, otherwise, receiving the narrative with remarkable calmness and attention.

"What the deuce is all this nonsense about the Stratford Town Council, and the penalties of the law?" cried Mr. Colebatch, when the carpenter had done. "But never mind; we can come to that afterwards. Now tell me about going back to get the mould out of the cupboard, and making the new cast. I know who did it. It's that dear, darling, incomparable little girl—but tell me all about it—come! quick, quick! don't keep me waiting!"

"Julius Cæsar" got on with his second narrative much more glibly than with the first. How Annie had suddenly remembered, one night, in her bed-room, about the mould having been left behind—how she was determined to try and restore her grand-father's health and faculties, by going to seek it; and how he (the carpenter) had gone also to protect her—how they got to Stratford, by the coach (outside places, in the cold, to save money)—how Annie appealed to the mercy of their former land lord, and instead of inventing some falsehood to deceive him, fairly told her whole story in all its truth—how the landlord pitied them, and promised to keep their secret—how they went up into the bedroom and found the mould in the old canvas bag, behind the volumes of the *Annual Register*, just where

Mr. Wray had left it—how Annie, remembering what her grand-father had told her about the process of making a cast, bought plaster, and followed out her instructions; failing in the first attempt, but admirably succeeding in the second—how they were obliged, in frightful suspense, to wait till the third day for the return coach; and how they finally got back, safe and sound, not only with the new cast, but with the mould as well. All these particulars flowed from the carpenter's lips, in a strain of homely eloquence, which no elocutionary aid could have furnished with one atom of additional effect, that would have done it any good whatever.

"We'd no notion, sir," said "Julius Cæsar," in conclusion, "that poor Mr. Wray was so bad as he really was, when we went away. It was a dreadful trial to Annie, sir, to go. She went down on her knees to the landlady—I saw her do it, half wild, like, she was in such a state—she went down on her knees, sir, to ask the woman to be as a daughter to the old man, till she came back. Well, sir, even after that, it was a toss-up whether she went away, when the morning came. But she was obliged to do it. She durstn't trust me to go alone, for fear I should let the mould tumble down, when I got it, (which I'm afraid, sir, was very likely)—or get into some scrape, by telling what I oughtn't, where I oughtn't; and so be taken up, mould and all, before the town council, who were going to put Mr. Wray in prison, only we ran off to Tidbury; and so—"

"Nonsense! stuff! they could no more put him in prison for taking the cast than I can," cried the Squire. "Stop! I've got a thought! I've got a thought at last, that's worth—is the mould here? Yes or no?"

"Yes, sir. Bless us and save us, what's the matter!"

"Run!" cried Mr. Colebatch, pacing up and down the room like mad. "No 15 in the street! Dabbs and Clutton, the lawyers! Fetch one of them in a second! Damn it, run! or I shall burst a blood-vessel!"

The carpenter ran *to* No 15; and Mr. Dabbs, who happened to be in, ran *from* No. 15. Mr. Colebatch met him at the street-door, dragged him into the back parlor, pushed him on to a chair, and instantly stated the case between Mr. Wray and the authorities at Stratford, in the fewest possible words and the hastiest possible tones. "Now," said the old gentleman at the end, "can they, or can they not, hurt him for what he's done?"

"It's a very nice point," said Mr. Dabbs, "a very nice point, indeed, sir."

"Hang it, man!" cried the Squire, "don't talk to *me* about 'nice points,' as if a point was something good to eat! Can they, or can they not, hurt him? Answer that in three words!"

"They can't," said Dabbs, answering it triumphantly in two.

"Why?" asked the Squire, beating him by a rejoinder in one.

"For this reason," said Dabbs. "What does Mr. Wray take with him into the church? Plaster of his own, in powder. What does he bring out with him? The same plaster, in another form. Does any right of copyright reside in a bust two hundred years old? Impossible. Has Mr. Wray hurt the bust? No; or they would have found him out here, and prosecuted directly—for they know where he is. I heard of the thing from a Stratford man, yesterday, who said they knew he was at Tidbury. Under all these circumstances, where's there a shadow of a case against Mr. Wray? Nowhere!"

"Capital, Dabbs! capital! you'll be Lord Chancellor some day; never heard a better opinion in my life! Now, Mr. Julius Caesar Blunt, do you see what my thought is? No! Look here. Take casts from that mould till your arms ache again; clap them upon slabs of black marble to show off the white face; sell them, at a guinea each, to the loads of people who would give anything to have a portrait of Shakspeare; and then open your breeches pockets fast enough to let the gold tumble in, if you can! Tell Mr. Wray that; and you tell him he's a rich man, or—no don't, you're no more fit to do it properly than I am! Tell every syllable you've heard here to Annie, directly; she'll know how to break it to him; go! be off!"

The Stolen Mask; or, The Mysterious Cash-Box

"But what are we to say about how we got the mould here, sir? We can't tell Mr. Wray the truth."

"Tell him a flam, of course! Say it's been found in the cupboard by the laudlord, at Stratford, and sent on here. Dabbs will bear witness that the Stratford people know he's at Tidbury, and know they can't touch him; he's sure to think *that* a pretty good proof that we are right. Say I bullied you out of the secret, when I saw the mould come here—say anything—but only go, and settle matters at once. I'm off to take my walk, and see about the black slabs at the stone-mason's. I'll be back in an hour, and see Mr. Wray."

The next moment, the impetuous old Squire was out of the house; and before the hour was up, he was in it again, rather more impetuous than ever.

When he entered the drawing-room, the first sight that greeted him was the carpenter, hanging up a box containing the mask, (with the lid taken off,) boldly and publicly, over the fire-place.

"I'm glad to see that, sir," said Mr. Colebatch shaking hands with Mr. Wray. "Annie has told you my good news—eh!"

"Yes, sir," answered the old man; "the best news I've heard for some time; I can hang up my treasure there, now, where I can see it all day. It was rather too bad, sir, of those Stratford people to go frightening me, by threatening what they couldn't do. The best man among them is the man who was my landlord; he's an honest, careful fellow, to send me back my old canvass bag and the mould, (which must have seemed worthless to him,) just because they were belonging to me, and left in my bed-room. I'm rather proud, sir, of making that mask. I can never repay you for your kindness in defending my character, and taking me up as you've done—but if you would accept a copy of the cast, now we have the mould to take it from, as Annie says—"

"That I will, and thankfully," said the Squire, "and I order five more copies, as presents to my friends, when you begin to sell to the public."

"I really don't know, sir, about that," said Mr. Wray, rather uneasily. "Selling the cast is like making my great treasure very common; it's like giving up my particular possession to everybody."

Mr. Colebatch parried this objection instantly. Could Mr. Wray, he asked, seriously mean to be so selfish as to deny to other lovers of Shakspeare the privilege he prized so much himself, of possessing Shakspeare's portrait—to say nothing of as good as plumply refusing a pretty round sum of money at the same time? Could he be selfish enough, and inconsiderate enough, to do that? No; Mr. Wray, on consideration, allowed he could not. He saw the subject in a new light now; and, begging Mr. Colebatch's pardon, if he had seemed selfish or unthankful, he would take the Squire's advice.

"That's right!" said the old gentleman. "Now I'm happy. You'll soon be strong enough, my good friend, to take the cast yourself."

"I hope so," said Mr. Wray. "It's very odd that a mere dream should make me feel so weak as I do—I suppose they told you, sir, what a horrible dream it was. If I didn't see the mask hanging up there now, as whole as ever, I should really believe it had been broken to pieces, just as I dreamt it. It must have been a dream, you know, sir, of course; for I dreamt that Annie had gone away and left me, and I found her at home as usual, when I woke up. It seems, too, that I'm a week or more behind-hand in my notion of the day of the month. In short, sir, I should almost think myself bewitched," he added, pressing his trembling hand over his forehead, "if I didn't know it was near Christmas time, and didn't believe what sweet Will Shakspeare says, in 'Hamlet'—a passage, by-the-by, sir, which Mr. Kemble always regretted to see struck out of the acting copy."

Here he began to declaim—faintly, but still with all the old Kemble cadences—the exquisite lines to which he referred; the Squire beating time to each modulation with his fore-finger:

"Some say, that ever 'gainst that season comes,
Wherein our Saviour's birth is celebrated,
This bird of dawning singeth all night long;
And 'then they say no spirit dares stir abroad;
The nights are wholesome; then no planets strike,
No fairy takes, nor witch hath power to charm,
So hallow'd and so gracious is the time."

"There's poetry!" exclaimed Mr. Colebatch, looking up at the mask. "That's a cut above my tragedy of the 'Mysterious Murderess,' I'm afraid. Eh, sir? And how you recite—splendid! Hang it! we havn't had half our talk, yet, about Shakespeare and John Kemble. A chat with an old stager like you is new life to me, in such a barbarous place as this! Ah! Mr. Wray, (and here the Squire's voice lowered and grew strangely tender for such a rough old gentleman,) "you are a happy man, to have a grand-child to keep you company at all times, but especially at Christmas time. I'm a lonely old bachelor, and must eat my Christmas dinner without wife or child to sweeten the taste to me of a single morsel!"

As little Annie heard this, she rose, and stole up to the Squire's side. Her pale face was covered with blushes (all her pretty natural color had not come back yet;) she looked softly at Mr. Colebatch, for a moment—then looked down—then said:

"Don't say you're lonely, sir! If you would let me be like a grand child to you, I should be so glad. I—I always make the plum-pudding, sir, on Christmas Day, for grand-father; if he would allow—and if—if you—"

"If that little love isn't trying to screw her courage up to ask me to taste her plum-pudding, I'm a Dutchman," cried the Squire, catching Annie in his arms, and fairly kissing her. "Without ceremony, Mr. Wray, I invite myself here to a Christmas dinner. We would have had it at Cropley Court; but you're not strong enough yet, to go out these cold nights. Never mind, all the dinner, except Annie's pudding, shall be done by my cook; Mrs. Buddle, the housekeeper, shall come and help; and we'll have such a feast, please God, as no king ever sat down to! No apologies, my good friend, on either side; I'm determined to spend the happiest Christmas Day I ever did in my life; and so shall you!"

And the good Squire kept his word. It was, of course, noised abroad over the whole town, that Matthew Colebatch, Esquire, Lord of the Manor of Tidbury-on-the-Marsh, was going to dine on Christmas Day with an old player, in a lodging-house. The genteel population were universally scandalized and indignant. The Squire had exhibited his leveling tendencies pretty often before, they said. He had, for instance, been seen cutting jokes in the High street with a traveling tinker, to whom he had applied in broad daylight to put a new ferule on his walking-stick; he had been detected coolly eating bacon and greens in one of his tenant farmer's cottages; he had been heard singing "Begone, dull care," in a cracked tenor, to amuse another tenant farmer's child. These actions were disreputable enough; but to go publicly, and dine with an obscure stage player, put the climax on everything! The Reverend Daubeny Daker said the Squire's proper sphere of action, after that, was a lunatic asylum; and the Reverend Daubeny Daker's friends echoed the sentiment.

Perfectly reckless of this expression of genteel popular opinion; Mr. Colebatch arrived to dinner at No. 12, on Christmas Day; and, what is more, wore his black tights and silk stockings, as if he had been going to a grand party. His dinner had arrived before him; and fat Mrs. Buddle, in her lavender silk gown, with a cambric handkerchief pinned in front to keep splashes off, appeared auspiciously with the banquet. Never did Annie feel the responsibility of having a plum-pudding to make, so acutely as she felt it, on seeing the savory feast which Mr. Colebatch had ordered, to accompany her one little item of saccharine cookery.

They sat down to dinner, with the Squire at the top of the table, (Mr. Wray insisted on that;) and Mrs. Buddle at the bottom, (he insisted on that also;) old Reuben and Annie, at one side; and "Julius Cæsar" all by himself (they knew his habits, and gave him elbow room,) at the other. Things were comparatively genteel and quiet, till Annie's pudding came in. At sight of that, Mr. Colebatch set up a cheer, as if he had been behind a pack of fox-hounds. The carpenter, thrown quite off his balance by noise and excitement, knocked down a spoon, a wine glass, and a pepper box, one after the other, in such quick succession, that Mrs. Buddle thought him mad; and Annie— for the first time, poor little thing, since all her troubles—actually began to laugh again, as prettily as ever. Mr. Colebatch did ample justice, it must be added, to her pudding. Twice did his plate travel up to the dish—a third time it would have gone; but the faithful housekeeper raised her warning voice, and reminded the old gentleman that he had a stomach.

When the tables were cleared, and the glasses filled with the Squire's rare old port, that excellent man rose slowly and solemnly from his chair, announcing that he had three toasts to propose, and one speech to make; the latter, he said, being contingent on the chance of his getting properly at his voice, through two helps of plum-pudding; a chance which he thought rather remote, principally in consequence of Annie's having rather overdone the proportion of suet in mixing her ingredients.

"The first toast," said the old gentleman, "is the health of Mr. Reuben Wray; and God bless him!" When this had been drunk with immense fervor, Mr. Colebatch went on at once to his second toast, without pausing to sit down—a custom which other after-dinner orators would do well to imitate.

"The second toast," said he, taking Mr. Wray's hand, and looking at the mask, which hung opposite, prettily decorated with holly—"the second toast, is a wide circulation and a hearty welcome all through England, for the Mask of Shakspeare!" This was duly honored; and immediately Mr. Colebatch went on like lightning to the third toast.

"The third," said he, "is the speech-toast." Here he endeavored, unsuccessfully, to cough up his voice out of the plum-pudding. "I say, ladies and gentlemen, this is the speech-toast." He stopped again, and desired the carpenter to pour him out a small glass of brandy; having swallowed which he went on fluently.

"Mr. Wray, sir," pursued the old gentleman, "I address you in particular, because you are particularly concerned in what I am going to say. Three days ago, I had a little talk in private with those two young people. Young people, sir, are never wholly free from some imprudent tendencies; and falling in love's one of them." (At this point, Annie slunk behind her grand father; the carpenter, having nobody to slink behind, put himself quite at his ease, by knocking down an orange.) "Now, sir," continued the Squire, "the private talk that I was speaking of, leads me to suppose that those two particular young people mean to marry each other. You, I understand, objected at first to their engagement; and like good and obedient children, they respected your objection. I think it's time to reward them for that, now. Let them marry, if they will, sir, while you can live happily to see it! I say nothing about our little darling there, but this—the vital question for her, and for all girls, is not how high, but how good, she, and they, marry. And I must confess, I don't think she's altogether chosen so badly." (The Squire hesitated a moment. He had in his mind, what he could not venture to speak— that the carpenter had saved old Reuben's life when the burglars were in the house; and that he had shown himself well worthy of Annie's confidence, when she asked him to aecompany her, in going to recover the mould from Stratford.) "In short, sir," Mr. Colebatch resumed—"to cut short speechifying, I don't think you can object to let them marry, provided they can find means of support. This, I think, they can do. First, there are the profits sure to come from the mask, which you are sure to share with them, I know." This prophecy about the profits was fulfilled; fifty copies of the cast were ordered by the new year; and they sold better still after that. "This will do to begin on, I think, Mr. Wray. Next, I intend to get our friend there a good berth as master-carpenter for the new Crescent they're going to build on my land, at the top of the hill—and that won't be a bad thing, I can tell you! Lastly, I mean you all to leave Tidbury, and live in a cottage of mine that's empty now, and going to rack and ruin for want of a tenant. I'll charge rent, mind, Mr. Wray, and come for it every quarter myself, as regular as a tax-gatherer. I don't insult an independent man by the offer of an asylum. Heaven forbid! but till you can do better, I want you to keep my cottage warm for me. I can't give up seeing my new grand-child sometimes, and I want my chat with an old stager, about the British drama and glorious John Kemble! To cut the thing short, sir; with such a prospect before them as this, do you object to my giving the healths of Mr. and Mrs. Martin Blunt that are to be!"

Conquered by the Squire's kind looks and words, as much as by his reasons, Old Reuben murmured approval of the toast, adding tenderly, as he looked round on Annie, "if she'll only promise always to let me live with her!"

"There, there!" cried Mr. Colebatch, "don't go kissing your grandfather before company like that, you little jade; making other people envious of him on Christmas Day! Listen to this! Mr. and Mrs. Martin Blunt that are to be—married in a week!" added the old gentleman, peremptorily.

"Lord, sir!" said Mrs. Buddle, "she can't get her dresses ready in that time!"

"She shall, ma'am, if every mantua-making wench in Tidbury stitches her fingers off for it, and there's an end of my speech-making!" Having said this, the Squire dropped back into his chair with a gasp of satisfaction.

"Now we are all happy!" he exclaimed, filling his glass; "and now we'll set in to enjoy our port in earnest—eh, my good friend?"

"Yes; all happy!" echoed old Reuben, patting Annie's hand, which lay in his; "but I think I should be still happier, though, if I could only manage not to remember that horrible dream!"

"Not remember it!" cried Mr. Colebatch, "we'll all remember it—all remember it together, from this time forth, in the same pleasant way!"

"How? How?" exclaimed Mr. Wray, eagerly.

"Why, my good friend!" answered the Squire, tapping him briskly on the shoulder "we'll all remember it gaily, as nothing but a *Story for a Christmas Fireside!*"

Lightning Source UK Ltd.
Milton Keynes UK
13 May 2010

154127UK00001B/346/P